"Ms. Mallory, This Is My Mostest Favorite Uncle Cuz He Always Keeps His Promises,"

Christy said, introducing her uncle to her teacher.

"I'm pleased to meet you." Kelly extended her hand.

"Chad Turner. It's my pleasure." His large hand seemed to envelop hers. "I wouldn't have minded having to stay in first grade for two years if you'd been my teacher."

Kelly looked at him, slightly puzzled. Children were seldom held back in first grade. Then she saw the mischievous twinkle in his eyes and quickly withdrew her hand. He must have been quite a devil when he was a child.

"My uncle was restrained in first grade. Burning kissability," Christy explained solemnly.

"Restrained for burning kissability?" Chad repeated, chuckling. His niece had a habit of completely mangling words she didn't understand.

He glanced at Kelly's bewildered expression. "Learning disability," he murmured.

"Oh," Kelly said inanely, preferring the literal meaning of Christy's words. The man's lips were definitely kissable....

Dear Reader:

Welcome! You hold in your hand a Silhouette Desire—your ticket to a whole new world of reading pleasure.

A Silhouette Desire is a sensuous, contemporary romance about passions, problems and the ultimate power of love. It is about today's woman—intelligent, successful, giving—but it is also the story of a romance between two people who are strong enough to follow their own individual paths, yet strong enough to compromise, as well.

These books are written by, for and about every woman that you are—wife, mother, sister, lover, daughter, career woman. A Silhouette Desire heroine must face the same challenges, achieve the same successes, in her story as you do in your own life.

The Silhouette reader is not afraid to enjoy herself. She knows when to take things seriously and when to indulge in a fantasy world. With six books a month, Silhouette Desire strives to meet her many moods, but each book is always a compelling love story.

Make a commitment to romance—go wild with Silhouette Desire!

Best,

Isabel Swift
Senior Editor & Editorial Coordinator

JO ANN ALGERMISSEN
Lucky Lady

Silhouette Desire

Published by Silhouette Books New York

America's Publisher of Contemporary Romance

SILHOUETTE BOOKS
300 East 42nd St., New York, N.Y. 10017

Copyright © 1988 by Jo Ann Algermissen

ISBN: 0-373-05409-2

First Silhouette Books printing March 1988

America's Publisher of Contemporary Romance

Printed in the U.S.A.

Books by Jo Ann Algermissen

Silhouette Desire

Naughty, but Nice #246
Challenge the Fates #276
Serendipity Samantha #300
Hank's Woman #318
Made in America #361
Lucky Lady #409

Silhouette Special Edition

Purple Diamonds #374

JO ANN ALGERMISSEN

believes in love, be it romantic love, sibling love, parental love or love of books. She's given and received them all. Ms. Algermissen and her husband of twenty years live on Kiawah Island in South Carolina with their two children, a weimaraner and three horses. She considers herself one lucky lady. Jo Ann also writes under the pseudonym Anna Hudson.

One

M*i* m*i*m will kill m*i* if I sl*i*sh h*i*me in the sn*i*w without b*i*ts," Christy Harvey said as she squirmed on Kelly Mallory's lap. "I j*i*st l*i*ve sn*i*w!"

Her mom will kill her if she sloshes home in the snow without boots, Kelly silently translated, struggling to pull a size four rubber boot over a size five shoe. *She loves snow.*

"Point your toe and shove your heel down," she instructed, determined that she would stretch the rubber boot thin enough to read a newspaper through rather than let Christy's shoes get wet.

Normally Kelly would have praised Christy for playing the magic vowel game by substituting the short *i* sound for every vowel spoken. Under different circumstances she would have been pleased to know her reading lessons were making a lasting impression, but at the moment she would have traded every successful teaching technique she knew for a larger pair of boots.

One minor problem had become an avalanche of problems coming faster than the snowflakes that were falling from the heavy clouds hovering over St. Louis. Five minutes ago the final bell had rung, and Christy's first-grade classmates had charged from the classroom, making a mad dash for the double doors at the end of the corridor. Twice in one day, she thought morosely, tugging with all her might.

Phillip Wadsworth, the new headmaster, had reprimanded her for not standing outside her door before school started. So what if her car had refused to start? So what if Christy's boots were too small? In his book, extenuating circumstances didn't exist. "Teacher supervision of the hallways is essential to maintaining discipline in the building," he had admonished her. She needed to "get her ducks in a row." Period.

Kelly glanced at the clock on the back wall as she jerked hard on the boot. Christy's bus would have departed by now. The thought of having to ask the headmaster to take the little girl home made her shudder.

"I'm going to get it this time!" Kelly clamped her teeth onto her lower lip. The boot snapped into place. "Finally!"

Christy jumped off her teacher's lap and inspected each boot. "N*it* m*i*ne," she said apologetically.

"They aren't yours?" Kelly couldn't believe her ears. "They have to be yours!"

"N*i*." Christy shrugged her thin shoulders as she took a second look and shook her head.

"Okay," Kelly said, and sighed in resignation. Glancing at the row of lockers lining the back of the room, she saw two slightly larger boots. Both pairs of boots did look the same at first glance. Taking a deep breath to calm herself, Kelly said, "You sit in the chair and we'll get these off cowboy-style."

Looking slightly puzzled, Christy obediently followed her teacher's directions by sitting in the chair and sticking one leg straight out.

Kelly turned her back to Christy and wedged the boot between her knees. "It shouldn't be as hard to remove them."

"But, Miz Mallory—" Christy patted Kelly on her backside. "Miz Mallory—"

"Quit squirming, sweetheart. I know you're anxious to get home so you can play in the snow. I'll have these off in a flash."

One quick yank later, the boot, with Christy's shoe still inside it, popped off the child's foot.

"Miz Mallory, I've been trying to tell you. It isn't my boot. It's my brother's old boots. Mommy gave my boots to my little sister."

Kelly straightened, fighting to keep control of her temper. Having been a middle child in a large family herself, and knowing how clothes were passed down regardless of fit, she was at last able to see the humor in the situation. This was one of those rare moments that could happen only in an elementary classroom.

A short burst of laughter escaped her lips. "Are these yours or not?"

"Nope, not really... just sort of." Christy giggled, and her bright blue eyes shone with surprise as she heard familiar laughter joining in. "Uncle Charming!" she shrieked, and flew across the room, one boot on and one boot off. "What are you doing here? Mom said you were baking your bones in the Florida sunshine!"

"I came home to help you build a snowman." The man who had been standing in the doorway tweaked her pug nose affectionately and winked flirtatiously at the little girl's attractive teacher.

"Remember? Last year I was in Mexico during the first snow and you made me promise to be here this year?"

Aptly named, Kelly mused, thinking of the nickname Christy had called her uncle. The little girl had chattered often about her favorite uncle. Although Kelly had never met him, she felt as though she knew "Uncle Charming" well. She watched him catch Christy and gently toss her into the air before giving her a bear hug. His wink, like an unexpected electrical charge, had made her heart skip a beat. Her instantaneous reaction reminded her of a lesson she'd learned long ago: Beware of handsome men with glib tongues. There was little doubt in her mind that "Uncle Charming" could charm the birds out of the trees, but Kelly had built herself a tidy, safe nest during the three years since her graduation. She wasn't about to fall out of that comfortable nest and break her heart again.

Vowing it would take more than sun-bleached blond hair, a winsome smile and a nice set of shoulders to change the course of her life, she steeled herself against the attraction she had initially felt toward him.

The man deposited Christy on the floor again, and the little girl turned to her teacher. "Miz Mallory, this is my mostest favorite uncle cuz he always keeps his promises. He's Mom's mostest favorite brother, too."

"I'm pleased to meet you," Kelly said, extending her hand.

"Chad Turner. My pleasure, I'm certain." His large hand seemed to envelop hers, and his dark brown eyes gazed appreciatively at Kelly. "I wouldn't have minded having to stay in first grade for two years if you'd been my teacher."

Skipping over his obvious flattery, Kelly looked at him, slightly puzzled. Children are seldom held back in first grade, she thought, but then saw the mischievous twinkle in his eyes and quickly withdrew her hand. He must have been quite a devil when he was a child.

"Uncle Charming was restrained in first grade. Burning kissability," Christy explained solemnly.

"Restrained for burning kissability?" Chad repeated, chuckling. His niece had a habit of completely mangling words she didn't understand.

"Something tells me you've been listening to adult conversations again."

Unrepentant for eavesdropping, Christy nodded. "Mom's voice sounded real sad."

Kelly had quickly translated "restrained" as a substitution for retained, but burning kissability was undecipherable. Mentally she ran through the alphabet searching for the correct letters. Concentrating on solving the puzzle, she didn't realize she was staring at Chad's jaunty smile.

Chad glanced at Kelly's puzzled expression and watched her lips move. "Learning disability."

"Oh," Kelly murmured inanely, preferring the literal meaning of Christy's words. His lips were definitely kissable.

Undaunted by having his past failures revealed, Chad took Christy's boot and teased, "I always got an E for effort when it came to putting on little girl's boots. Let's see if I've still got the knack."

Giggling, Christy let her uncle lift her onto the reading table. "My shoe's inside the boot."

"Hmmm." Chad peeked inside the boot. "Loafers. I think we'll leave the shoe in the boot and slip your foot inside. Ready?"

Kelly stood back, wondering why she hadn't thought of that simple solution. She began clearing her desk as Christy and her uncle struggled with the boot. She had one stop to make and then she could go home, climb into bed and pull the covers over her head. This was one day she wanted to be done with as quickly as possible.

"Miz Mallory needs a ride," Christy announced, grabbing Chad's shoulders to keep from sliding backward on the Formica tabletop. Her foot slid inside her shoe. "Her car is broken."

Helpfulness and generosity were lovable traits most six-year-olds shared but at the moment Kelly wished Christy had kept her mouth closed. Kelly rarely asked for favors. Although she constantly helped others, she disliked feeling indebted to anyone.

Before Chad could respond, Kelly said, "I have to stop by Todd's house."

"Todd has a broken leg," Christy explained to her uncle. "Miz Mallory tulips him."

"Tutors," Kelly corrected, grinning.

Chad straightened, returning her smile. "No problem. We'll take Christy and her brothers home and while they start building the snowman I'll take you to your student's house. How long will you be there?"

"Half an hour, but—"

"Good. That will give me time to finish the snowman. I'll pick you up and take you home."

His offer was tempting. On a Friday afternoon during a blinding snowstorm, the chances of hailing a taxi would be almost nonexistent. She dreaded the prospect of trudging through the snow to Todd's house, then tramping another mile home.

Kelly paused long enough for Chad to misconstrue her silence as acceptance. He reached toward her to remove the books she had clutched against her chest almost as a protective barrier. The back of his arm accidentally touched hers, and she stepped backward, keeping the books firmly in place. Aware that she was overreacting to his slight touch, Kelly felt her face turn crimson. Warning lights flashing in her mind prompted a firm refusal. "Thanks, but I like walking in the snow."

"Nonsense," Chad scoffed, noticing her heightened color, which accentuated the enchanting spray of freckles across the bridge of her nose. For some reason, her reluctance to accept his cordial offer upset him. "Underneath the snow there's an icy glaze. Unless you have spikes on your boots, you won't be safe on those slick sidewalks."

"I'll manage," she replied in a schoolmarmish voice that brooked no refusal. Realizing she'd been a bit abrupt, Kelly smiled politely and added, "I appreciate the kind offer."

The last thing she needed to round off her day would be for Christy's uncle to file a complaint with the headmaster. She'd violated enough rules for one day. Phillip would consider rudeness an intolerable breach of protocol, and in an expensive private school like this one, that was a serious offense.

"Anybody ever tell you that female independence can result in frostbitten toes?" Chad asked teasingly.

Ignoring his gibe, she stooped down, buttoned Christy's coat, straightened the little girl's wool scarf and gave her a swift hug. "You have fun this weekend. I'll see you Monday."

Chad studied his niece's teacher, noting the genuine affection between woman and child. He couldn't force her to accept a ride, but leaving her stranded bothered him. Removing a sheet of paper from the notepad in his breast pocket, he hastily wrote down two phone numbers.

"C'mon, Uncle Chad." Christy slipped her mitten-covered hand into his. "Don't argue with Miz Mallory. You'll get me in trouble."

Smiling lazily, he tucked the slip of paper between the pages of one of Kelly's books, saying, "Call me if you need a ride."

"Nice meeting you, Mr. Turner," she replied courteously.

"See you."

Kelly's blue eyes met his. Some subtle current passed between them, lending his parting words significance. She shook her head to break the invisible threads threatening to bind her. Turning, she moved behind her desk.

Long moments after they'd left, Kelly found herself inhaling deeply. At twenty-six, she wasn't supposed to act like a gawky teenager mooning over every handsome male she saw. Silently chastising herself, she finished clearing off her desk. She neatly placed her lesson plan book on the desktop and glanced warily toward the door when she heard the sound of footsteps approaching. One dose of Chad Turner's considerable charm was her limit.

When Trudy Lane entered her classroom, Kelly didn't know if she felt relief or disappointment.

"Was that Christy's father?" Trudy asked, as if it were a matter of great concern.

"No, Christy's uncle." Kelly rolled her eyes in mock despair when Trudy shook her fingertips as though they were on fire. Most of the time, Trudy's reactions amused her. Her friend had a highly developed interest in handsome men and made no bones about it. From the beginning, Trudy had told her that teaching kindergarten was a stopgap between college and marriage. Her first priority in life was finding a husband; her second priority was having children of her own. Switching the subject away from Chad Turner to Trudy's favorite topic, Kelly asked, "Big plans with Richard for the weekend?"

"Richard? Richard who?" Trudy asked teasingly. "Is he married?" she demanded, obviously referring to Chad Turner.

Kelly lifted her shoulders. "I didn't ask."

"You have eyes. Was he wearing a ring?"

"I didn't notice."

Slumping into Kelly's chair, Trudy shook her head in disbelief. "A handsome man wanders into the Desert of Available Males and she doesn't notice whether he's wearing a ring or not? I swear, lady, you'd refuse to drink from an oasis because you'd be certain it was a mirage. What am I going to do with you?"

"Let me die of thirst peacefully, I hope," Kelly responded, knowing Trudy's third priority in life was finding a Prince Charming for her best friend. Grinning, she wondered what Trudy would say if she heard Christy's nickname for her uncle.

"What are you smirking about? You're not holding back on your old buddy, are you? Did he ask you for a date?"

"I'm not smirking or holding out on you. He didn't ask me for a date."

Trudy groaned. "You're hopeless."

"Humph! Yesterday you called me a chump. My dear, I think the kids are getting to you. Name-calling is strictly kindergarten stuff."

"As far as I'm concerned, volunteering to do the front-hall bulletin board when it's Priscilla's turn qualifies you as a chump."

"Priscilla is busy organizing the sixth-grade Thanksgiving feast." Much preferring to discuss her supposed character weakness rather than to continue having Trudy drill her about Christy's uncle, she added, "I don't mind doing the bulletin board."

The dreamy expression on Trudy's face indicated the failure of Kelly's diversionary tactic.

"He has a beautiful tan. Must be nice to winter where the sun is shining. Where do you suppose he's been?"

"Florida."

"Florida! According to the television commercials, they make their own rules in Florida. Fun in the sun. No clocks. No work."

"No paycheck," Kelly inserted matter-of-factly, but she glanced outside and shivered. Like tens of thousands of other Missourians, she sometimes longed for a warmer climate.

Trudy straightened. "Right. No paycheck. Without a paycheck, I'd have to live the life of a beach bum—" she grinned "—or find myself a rich man who winters in Florida. You didn't happen to get that handsome hunk's name, address and phone number, did you?"

"Trudy, get serious. If I did get that information, you wouldn't use it."

"Wouldn't I? It's time you faced the hard, cruel facts, Kelly. Neither one of us is getting any younger. Before you know it, we'll be collecting social security and searching for a retirement home for aged spinsters."

Kelly chuckled. "That serious, huh? Well, I guess as soon as the snow melts we'd better start shuffleboard practice."

"Ha-ha, not funny. I don't know about you, but I know I'm beginning to get desperate. The other afternoon I caught myself staring at Phillip Wadsworth when he was on hall patrol. Even he is beginning to look good."

"There's nothing wrong with Phillip."

"Give me a break, Kelly. He's S-T-U-F-F-Y! Spelled in capital letters."

"Sounds like a perfect match—the stuffy headmaster and the decrepit spinster."

"See! I'm not the only one near the breaking point. He's beginning to look good to you, too."

"He's . . . safe."

"So's a hot-water bottle, but that doesn't mean I want to share my bed with one permanently."

"He's settled."

"As in rut," Trudy agreed, faking a yawn.

"He's secure."

"Safe, settled and secure," Trudy repeated, hissing the first letter of each word. She jumped from the chair and began waving her arms. "Phillip Wadsworth is meat and potatoes. Your blond visitor looks like champagne and caviar—wild and wonderful! I'll settle for a bland diet when I'm pushing ninety from the other side!"

"A steady diet of champagne and caviar might leave a bitter aftertaste," Kelly said, unwilling to let Trudy have the last word.

She moved to her coat locker, remembering that Todd was eagerly awaiting her arrival. Trudy watched her friend ease her arms into her puffy down-filled coat, then change from serviceable rubber-soled shoes into knee-high boots. Kelly pulled an unflattering wool stocking hat over her auburn hair until it covered her ears. "Your eating habits match your clothing—practical but unexciting."

"I'll take that as a compliment," Kelly replied, casting her outspoken friend a cheeky smile.

"It wasn't meant as one," Trudy grumbled. "I suppose you're on your way to Todd's house?"

"Yeah." A slight frown wrinkled her brow as she thought of Todd. Handicapped by being dyslexic, he needed all the extra help he could get. "I don't want him to get further behind than he already is. He's already frustrated."

"Chump."

Pulling on the mittens that matched her cap, Kelly automatically straightened the row of desks as she moved to the front of the room. "Dedicated."

"Todd's parents could afford a private tutor. They're taking advantage of you."

"I don't mind," she said truthfully. Todd was a challenge. She was determined to teach him to read, no matter how difficult that task proved to be. For an instant she wondered if the reason Chad Turner had been retained in first grade was that he was dyslexic, too. It was a common problem. Refusing to let her thoughts linger on Uncle Charming, she lengthened her stride. "Hand me the brown envelope in the bottom drawer, would you?"

Nodding, Trudy opened the drawer and pulled out the bulky package. "Need a ride?"

"Todd's house is in the opposite direction from yours." Kelly hated the thought of imposing. The way her luck was running, they would probably both get stuck in a snowbank.

"I should have known better than to ask," Trudy groaned. "You say yes when you should say no, and no when you should say yes. Don't argue. I'll meet you at the time clock in the office."

Kelly grimaced, certain she was going to be told to get her ducks in a row twice in one day. The chance that the headmaster had missed seeing her students race from her classroom was slim. After supervising class dismissal, Phillip made a habit of keeping an eye on the checkout clock: he measured dedication in hours and minutes.

Impulsively she considered asking Trudy to clock out for her, but decided against it. If Phillip caught Trudy, that would be a major infraction of his newly imposed rules. They'd both be in trouble.

"Or," Trudy added when she saw Kelly's scowl, "if you're running late, you can clock me out and I'll meet you at the car."

"Good idea, but it's against the rules. Phillip is already displeased with me. My arriving seconds before the late bell rang this morning and letting the kids run down the corridor after school didn't chalk up any brownie points on the positive side of my evaluation sheet."

Trudy started for the door, pausing long enough to get the last word. "Good teachers shouldn't have to worry about brownie points. Wadsworth should be thanking his lucky stars that you're on staff. Every elementary school needs one resident chump to do the dirty work. If he doesn't appreciate you, tell him to kiss off."

She was gone before Kelly could think of a flip reply. Picking up the stack of paperwork she had to grade over the weekend, she worried her lower lip with her teeth. Just once, she mused, I wish I had the nerve to tell somebody—anybody—to kiss off.

The slang expression brought a smile to her lips. She wasn't certain she knew exactly what it meant. "Kiss off," she muttered, somewhat surprised that she liked the sound of it.

Phillip would be shocked if he overheard me, she thought, glancing warily from side to side down the empty corridor. Reassured that no one was there, she proceeded toward the office.

Talking to Trudy often tempted Kelly to reexamine her don't-make-waves philosophy. She'd often admired her friend's I'll-spit-in-your-eye-before-you-see-me-cry attitude. On the rare occasions when Kelly hadn't managed to hold on to what her brothers called her redheaded temper, she'd let a few cutting remarks mar her record of self-discipline.

Yeah, and you had guilt attacks for days afterward, she reminded herself.

Her family was never far from her thoughts. Her mother had passed away when Kelly was in her early teens, and her father had recently retired and moved away. Her three older brothers and two younger sisters were married and living on their own, but they were still a close-knit family. In fact, her family were the only people who'd seen Kelly really angry.

Soon after her mother died, Kelly had learned not to make waves. As in most large families, there were frequent minor squabbles, with all the siblings choosing sides in an instant. Often these squabbles had erupted into major warfare. Being the oldest girl in the family, she'd had to assume the role of surrogate mother, and inevitably after the battle she'd felt emotionally battered and bruised. It didn't take long for her to realize she could avoid confrontation by playing the role of peacemaker before things got out of hand.

Peacemaker, she mused, deciding to correct Trudy's mistaken impression of her. Being cooperative and diplomatic was very different from being a chump, she thought. Many a time her brothers and sisters had crowded around her as she'd flipped a coin to decide who'd do what without fighting. Being the family arbitrator had made her important. What did that have to do with being a chump? she asked herself defiantly.

Kelly shook her head slightly, as if to clear it. No, she thought, refusing to see herself in an unflattering light. Peacemakers, like diplomats, were held in high esteem by everyone.

Being a middle child was never easy, but she'd survived with her self-esteem intact because of a simple question she seldom minded asking: *What can I do to please you?*

As the distance between her classroom and the office narrowed, she wondered what she could do to help Phillip Wadsworth that would make him forget about her minor infraction of the administration's rules. There had to be something she could do to placate him. After all, despite what Trudy had said, he wasn't an ogre. He was just doing his job.

As she turned the corner and headed toward the attendance office, she saw Phillip and Priscilla engaged in deep conversation down the corridor. See? she thought, smiling. Good deeds are rewarded. With luck, she'd be in and out of the office before Phillip caught sight of her.

Walking as quietly as possible, Kelly hurried into the office and removed her time card from the long rack. She inadvertently jumped when the machine loudly printed the checkout time on her card. Glancing at the rack again, she resisted the temptation to punch Trudy out, too. Leaning forward, Kelly peeked through the office window, praying Trudy would arrive promptly. If her luck held, she'd be long gone before Phillip returned to his office.

Two

Kelly ducked back from the window when she heard Phillip's voice echoing in the empty corridor. He seemed to be coming closer and closer. Pretending to study the school calendar hanging on the wall, she tried to think of a peace offering that would make him think she had her ducks in a straight line. There had to be something she could do to please him.

She raised the page. "December," she muttered, her eyes drawn to the date circled in red. "Christmas!"

Within an instant she had an idea that was certain to please Phillip. No one in her right mind would volunteer to direct the Christmas program. Last year she'd sworn never to do it again.

She heard the rhythmic tapping of Priscilla's high heels. Turning, she beamed Phillip a smile guaranteed to deflect the sternest glare. "Less than a month until the Christmas program. Who's going to direct it this year?"

Phillip opened his mouth, but Priscilla quickly said, "Kelly did a marvelous job last year. The parents gave her rave reviews."

The parents raved; I went stark raving crazy, Kelly remembered. The kids had looked angelic the night of the program, but they'd been absolute devils during the rehearsals.

Kelly did her best to hide her fear of being chastised behind the perpetual smile she maintained when in the presence of the headmaster. Priscilla was the only teacher who hadn't commented on the success of last year's pageant until now, she realized. She wondered if Phillip was aware that the responsibility for the program alternated between the primary grades and the upper grades, and that by all rights it should be Priscilla's turn this year. Her smile slipped a notch as she realized the ulterior motive behind her colleague's compliment.

Determined to be gracious, she replied, "Thanks, Priscilla."

Trudy had waltzed into the office in time to hear Priscilla's remark. Barging between the headmaster and the sixth-grade teacher, she shot Kelly a meaningful glare. "Isn't it *marvelous* that the upper grades are scheduled to do the program this year? Who's going to direct it? Priscilla?"

"Oh, I couldn't," Priscilla demurred. "My head swims at the thought of putting together an elaborate program."

"I enjoyed—"

Kelly stopped midsentence when Trudy stepped heavily on her toe. The look in her eyes squelched the remainder of Kelly's offer. "Oh, sorry, Kelly. Ready to leave?"

"This early?" Phillip's disapproval was more than obvious as he glanced at his watch.

"On Friday Kelly tutors the boy in her class who broke his leg," Trudy explained. "Since the weather is so nasty, I'm driving her over there."

Kelly saw the defiant expression on Trudy's face and heard the if-you-don't-like-it-kiss-off ring in her voice. Priscilla looked shocked. Phillip looked as if he didn't believe Trudy's words and suspected the two teachers were skirting their duties.

"I'll be happy to help with the Christmas program," Kelly volunteered, blocking the hostile glance Trudy aimed at Phillip by stepping between them. Shifting her homework into one arm she began to push Trudy to the door. "It should be fun working with the older children for a change."

"Terrific!" Priscilla cheered, obviously glad to be relieved of the responsibility.

"Yeah, terrific," Trudy grudgingly seconded, shaking her head in disbelief. All her protective efforts had been in vain. "Come on, Kelly, before you volunteer to clean the building over the weekend!"

Kelly ventured a glance upward. Phillip wasn't smiling, exactly, but at least he wasn't scowling. Taking that as a promising sign, she said, "Have a nice weekend. See you Monday—bright and early," she tacked on for good measure.

"Early will do nicely," Phillip replied pointedly.

Although they appeared to be marching down the hallway side by side, Kelly was loping along to keep up with Trudy's angry strides. They reached to push the door open at the same time.

"Allow me," Trudy said angrily. "Your arms are full."

An icy gust of wind hit Kelly. She shivered.

"Watch out for those steps. There must be an inch of ice under this stuff," Kelly said, burying her nose in the collar of her coat until only her eyes were showing. She knew she'd annoyed Trudy by volunteering, but at least she'd avoided being reprimanded by Phillip. She'd also protected her friend from being insubordinate on her behalf. Hoping to placate Trudy, she said, "Why don't you come to my place for dinner?"

"No, thanks. The last time you invited me over I watched the boob tube while you graded papers. That's not my idea of how to spend a fun-filled Friday evening."

"I'll fix scampi," she said cajolingly as she navigated her way down the slippery steps. "Stuffed artichokes."

"Bribery won't work."

"Strawberry cheesecake?" A snowflake caught in her eyelashes. "Better yet, snowflake ice cream. My sisters and I used to make it when we were kids. You'll love it."

"Food won't absolve you from guilt, Kelly Mallory. You knew I was doing everything but clamping my hand over your mouth to keep you from volunteering to direct the Christmas program. I'm beginning to think you have masochistic tendencies."

Kelly dusted the snow from Trudy's rear window with her gloved hand. "Hand me the scraper and I'll get the windows for you."

"For Pete's sake, Kelly, your arms are full. I'll scrape the windows. You get in the car!"

As she did as she was told, Kelly could hear her friend grumbling about what had taken place in the office. Trudy is wrong, she thought, settling against the stiff vinyl seat. She hadn't volunteered because she was a masochist. Masochist's liked pain; she had simply avoided Phillip's criticism by volunteering. Regardless of how Trudy interpreted her actions, Kelly knew she'd done the right thing. She'd made Phillip and Priscilla happy. Trudy wasn't overjoyed, but what the heck, two out of three wasn't bad.

She'd learned from dealing with her brothers and sisters that she couldn't always make everybody happy. Sometimes she had had to be content with having the majority of her family at peace.

"I promise not to grade papers while you're at my place," Kelly said when Trudy slid into the driver's seat. "Don't be angry with me."

For a long moment, Trudy stared at Kelly; then she started the car's engine. "You make it tough to stay mad."

Kelly squirmed when she heard Trudy's deep sigh.

"You can quit wiggling around. I'm not going to lecture you." Trudy's mouth twisted into a grim smile. "Although if anyone ever needed a lecture, it's you."

"Thanks." Kelly grinned. "I knew you'd understand."

"Understand? Yes. Approve? No." She shifted gears and eased the car forward over a snowdrift. "I'll take you up on your dinner invitation during the week. Tonight Nose-to-the-Grindstone George is supposed to take me to the symphony. Two bits says he won't have enough courage to get out in this snowstorm. He'll probably walk from his apartment to mine and want to spend the evening drinking soda and popping popcorn. Ugh! Why are all the stick-in-the-muds attracted to me? Why can't I get someone with a gorgeous Florida suntan?"

Kelly gasped when the car began to skid. "Opposites attract?" she managed to say.

Trudy spun the steering wheel skillfully until the car righted itself. "Yeah, I guess."

Curious, Kelly asked, "Why are you dating George if you don't enjoy being with him?"

"Romantic optimism. I figure if I kiss enough frogs one of them will turn into a prince!"

Chuckling, Kelly pointed to an upcoming street. "Turn right. Todd's house is the third drive on the left." Sizing up the steep incline leading to the Georgian mansion, she added, "Maybe you should drop me off at the bottom of the hill."

Ignoring the suggestion, Trudy turned into the circular drive. Halfway up the hill, the wheels spun madly and the car slowed to a slippery halt. "Leave your homework with me. I'll drop it off at your place."

"Are you sure you don't mind?" Trudy's apartment was close to the small house Kelly rented, but she hated the thought of her friend having to make an extra stop. She'd already gone three blocks out of her way.

"No problem. Call me if you need a ride home."

Without replying, Kelly opened the car door. She planted one foot in the bank of snow edging the drive, stood and gave Trudy a hasty wave while struggling to maintain her balance. The wind whistled around her as she watched until Trudy had safely backed down the drive, grateful to have such a good friend.

Uncertain whether the snowbank or the icy pavement would yield the best footing, she tucked the brown envelope under her arm and opted for the deeper snow. Despite her heavy coat, gloves and boots, by the time she stood on the wide front porch stomping her feet, she was shivering.

"Miz Mallory!" Todd, standing with the aid of his crutches, opened the door before she rang the bell. "I knew you wouldn't forget me!"

Kelly grinned as she stepped into the foyer. The young boy's smile made all the trials and tribulations of being a teacher worthwhile, she thought. Kelly knew she was one of the most important people in his life.

An hour later Kelly had to remind herself of that thought. Due to the road conditions and a jackknifed eighteen-wheeler on the innerbelt, Todd's father hadn't arrived home. His mother had offered to drive her home, but the live-in housekeeper had left for the weekend. Kelly knew Todd's mother was reluctant to take her son along, but she was equally hesitant to leave him home alone while taking a chance of getting stranded. After trying in vain to call a cab, Kelly convinced both mother and son that she loved walking in the snow on a wintry evening.

She'd only forgotten one small item.

Two weeks ago, when she'd first visited Todd at home, he'd shown her his six-week-old mongrel puppies and begged her to take one rather than let it be taken to the Humane Society. Reluctantly she'd promised to find a home for the puppy or take it herself.

She'd forgotten about it, but Todd hadn't.

At the end of the lesson he'd brought out a box with the puppy snuggled inside beneath a worn blanket. Dismayed, she'd hesitated, considering the consequences of refusing, but one tear brimming in Todd's blue eyes had made saying no almost impossible. Chin wobbling, he'd reminded her that she had promised to take Mr. Wiggles. Her fate was sealed.

Now, holding the cardboard box containing the pup, who was wrapped tightly in a blanket, she navigated the treacherous road that ran in front of the school. Todd's tears had led her to make an unwise decision, she knew. She should have simply arranged to take the puppy at a later date.

"Like when my car's fixed. Or when I've found a good home for him. Maybe I am a chump," she muttered. The box shifted as the dog moved, whimpering in response to the sound of her voice. "What do you think, Mr. Wiggles?"

If silence meant agreement, the dog concurred. His whimpering stopped.

Kelly glanced down the hill at the school, hoping at least one of the teachers had stayed late despite the weather. But the parking lot was empty, and there were no lights on. Looking toward the building, she missed a patch of ice covering a puddle.

"Ooooooh!" Her right foot slid out from under her. "Whooooa!" The left foot followed. She felt herself falling face forward.

Mr. Wiggles yelped, his sharp claws making a scratching noise on the cardboard. The box almost fell from her grip.

Thoughts racing as she kept the box upright, she knew her first responsibility was Mr. Wiggles's safety. She'd never be able to face Todd if anything happened to the puppy. She managed to hold the box, even when her face hit the snow.

Spread-eagled on the ground, she gave a low groan. The puppy was safe, but she wasn't too sure about herself. There were moments in her adult life when she wanted to roll over and childishly bang her heels on the ground, and this was one of them.

Mr. Wiggles yelped and managed to climb out of the box. His black button nose sniffed around Kelly's face, and then he gave her several wet dog kisses.

Finally she lifted one snow-caked eyelid. "You love me, huh?"

Wiggles wagged his short, stubby tail until his whole rear end was in motion. Like any other small creature that has been confined, he wanted to play now that he was free. He bounced forward and grabbed the woolen scarf around her neck.

Kelly couldn't help but laugh when Wiggles dug his back feet into the snow and growled. She grabbed her scarf and tugged. "Recess? You think it's time to play tug-of-war, huh?"

His tail wagged harder, something Kelly wouldn't have thought possible. Dropping his hold on her scarf, he cocked his head to one side and stared at her. An instant later, he lost interest in the tug-of-war and bounded from one snowdrift to the next.

"Oh, no, you don't." Kelly scrambled to her feet. "Come back here, Wiggles. I'm not chasing you around the schoolyard. Here, boy. C'mon."

The little dog began to shake slightly, as if feeling the cold for the first time, but still moved across the crust forming on the snow. He skittered down the hillside, then charged back to Kelly's side.

She stooped to pick him up, he but dodged backward. "C'mon, you rascal," she coaxed. "Let's go home where it's toasty warm. I know you're getting cold. We'll play there. How'd you like a nice hot bowl of milk, hmm?"

Wiggles yelped and circled her, barely keeping out of reach. Each time she tried to catch him he leaped farther backward. Annoyed, she shook her finger at him and said in her best schoolmarm's voice, "Wiggles, you get over here right now!"

The puppy had the good grace to cower for a moment, then dashed wildly over the snowbanks lining the street. Kelly automatically looked both ways before chasing him. A car cresting the hill blinked its lights. Wiggles froze dead center in the street.

"Wiggles!"

Kelly plunged into the street. The headlights were only yards away when she grabbed the puppy and rolled to the curb. Huddled with Wiggles against her chest, she shook with fright. She didn't even see the car skid to a halt or hear the car door open.

"Good God almighty, woman!" a masculine voice boomed. "What are you trying to do? Get yourself killed?"

That she did hear. She recognized the voice, too. Chad Turner.

She felt herself being lifted and shaken at the same time, and none too gently.

"Are you hurt?"

"No." Her teeth were chattering like castanets. "But ... you nearly ... hit Wiggles."

"I nearly hit both of you!" Chad had been in a multitude of close calls during his youth, but he couldn't remember ever having been as scared or angry as he was now. "Didn't you realize the car was out of control? I could have run over you!"

His biting tone hurt worse than the fingers he'd dug into her upper arms. He didn't have to berate her for saving her dog. Granted, she'd acted impulsively and perhaps unwisely, but that didn't give him the right to chew on her. Hadn't she been through enough for one day?

"K-k-kissss off-f-f!"

"What?"

She looked him square in the eye and said, clearly and firmly, "Kiss off."

"That's what I thought you said. Christy got her mouth washed out with soap for using that phrase. Now that I know where it came from, I'm tempted to do the same for you."

Anger heated her face, making it tingle. You and whose army? she wanted to demand, but she clamped her teeth together and tucked the shivering puppy inside her coat. She'd already shredded her dignity by rolling in front of his car and letting her redheaded temper get control of her tongue. She wasn't going to lose what dignity she had left by standing in the middle of an ice-covered street swapping insults.

"Excuse me!" she said, brushing past him and striding off. She shivered as the ice on Wiggles's paws began to melt and soak through her clothes. She thought she'd had the last word until she felt her feet leave the icy pavement. In one effortless swoop he'd pinned her against his camel hair coat. "Put me down this instant!" she yelled.

"Why? So you and your dog can go play in the traffic again. Nope. I'm taking you home."

"I'm safer walking in the middle of the street than I am riding with a man who loses control of his car," she countered.

Wiggles stuck his nose out from under her coat and issued a puny, halfhearted growl.

"Shut up, dog."

"Don't you tell my dog to shut up."

"Okay, I won't. You shut up!"

With that he opened the passenger door and dumped her inside. Eyes narrowed, Kelly watched him pass in front of the car. She almost felt like shifting the car into gear and goosing the accelerator. Let him see how if feels to play tag with a moving vehicle, she thought vengefully.

She also considered getting out of the car and leaving his obnoxious presence. She'd walked this far. Another mile or so wouldn't kill her. She certainly wasn't going to accept a ride from a man who thought she had some kind of bizarre death wish. She reached for the door handle.

"Don't," Chad warned as he got into the driver's seat. "You open that door and I'll be on you like fleas on Rover."

"How charming," she commented with frigid sarcasm. Uncle Charming. Humph! Uncle Ugly would have been more appropriate. Most first-graders were good judges of character, but obviously Christy was the exception that proved the rule. Prim to the bone, she added, "I will accept your offer of a ride home, but only for the sake of the puppy."

Chad gripped the steering wheel until his knuckles turned white. This was the woman he'd felt attracted to earlier? This was the woman with the warm laughter and the spontaneous hugs? This was the woman who'd intrigued him enough to make him leave the warmth of his sister's home to find her and give her a ride? He'd pulled some crazy stunts in his life, but this one was a record-breaker.

"Where does Fido live?" he asked, struggling to keep his voice emotionless.

Where does Fido live? she silently repeated. Smart aleck. She had an older brother, Tom, who was exactly like Chad Turner. Charm oozed out of his pores when it suited him. When it didn't, Tom could be a complete nincompoop, smart mouth and all. There was no pleasing him when he was in one of his moods. Oh, sure, Tom had more girls' names in his little black book than his brothers ever had, but he was her only sibling who could rub her the wrong way without even trying. Strange, the effect that had on her. It made her try harder, offer to do more. She refused him nothing to gain his approval.

Kelly hugged Wiggles closer. Tom and Chad Turner were two different people. Chad wasn't part of her family. She wouldn't let him needle her.

"Go three blocks, turn left. *Mr. Wiggles's* house is the fifth one on the left side of the street."

Chad nodded, not trusting himself to make a civil comment. After several moments of silence, he said, "I suppose Spot has a bowl of puppy food waiting for him at home."

"A warm bowl of milk should do nicely," she replied sweetly. "Thank you kindly for your concern."

"If I had a puppy—" He stopped in midsentence, then glanced at the bulge straining the buttons on her coat.

From the tone of his voice, Kelly deduced that Chad wouldn't feed his dog warm milk. Defensively she asked, "What's wrong with warm milk? It's very nutritious."

"Nothing. You're the one who'll have to clean up after him."

"He's just been weaned. Warm milk should be perfect." She watched Chad casually lift one shoulder, as though saying, I warned you. But you're too hardheaded to listen.

"I've never raised a puppy," she admitted. The Mallorys had had enough mouths to feed without adding any pets. "I guess you raised lots of dogs?"

"Dozens."

"No warm milk, huh?"

"Not unless your puppy has made history by being the first successful crossbreed between a cow and a dog." Chad turned the corner and began counting the houses. "One, two, three . . ."

The nearest convenience store was six blocks away.

"Four . . ."

She hated asking favors from anyone, and yet she knew she was about to ask Uncle Ugly to drive her to the store. She couldn't let the puppy starve or feed it something that would make it sick. She opened her mouth to speak.

"Five." He drove past the driveway. "Was that Killer's new home?"

"Yes."

"There's a Quick Shop on Olive Boulevard, isn't there?"

"Yes, but . . ."

Chad slowed the car as he neared the stop sign at the end of the block. "But what?"

"I hate inconveniencing you," she replied bluntly.

Glancing to the left, then to the right, for road clearance, he let his eyes linger momentarily on the small woman huddled against the door. By rights he should have dropped her off at her house. She hadn't shown a smidgen of gratitude for being rescued from freezing to death. If anything, she'd been downright antagonistic.

"Why?" he muttered. Why was he bothering to be nice to a woman who seemed to detest him for no reason? What was there about Kelly Mallory that made him want to make certain she got home safe and sound?

She's Christy's teacher, he told himself, knowing that had little to do with the truth.

Several teachers' names headed his Least Favorite People list. He'd never been teacher's pet. Mutual animosity best described the relationships he'd had with most of his teachers.

Was that why he was trying to impress Christy's teacher? he wondered. Was the peculiar sensation he felt in the pit of his stomach when he looked at Kelly some sort of long-delayed reaction to having his self-esteem trampled into the dirt at an early age?

Could be, he mused, remembering the apprehension he'd felt that afternoon when he'd walked into the school building. Taffy, a dog he'd had as a child, who'd been hit by a car as a puppy, had had a similar reaction every time she'd entered the animal hospital. One whiff of the antiseptic smell and Taffy would sit on her rump and stubbornly refuse to budge. Despite the vet's gentle care, Taffy never forgot the old pain.

He hadn't forgotten, either. Years of being successful hadn't obliterated his old insecurities.

Good grief, Chad thought, was my reason for going out into a blizzard simply a desire to please a teacher? At thirty-two he was too damned old to start polishing apples for the teacher now!

"Why?" Kelly worried her lower lip between her teeth. She hadn't expected him to ask for an explanation. "I guess I prefer being self-reliant."

Chad inched his Mercedes across the rutted intersection. "Do you teach self-reliance to your students?" he asked, baiting her.

"Of course."

"Of course," he repeated, taking perverse delight in agreeing with her, but knowing she was wrong. If Kelly practiced what she preached, he told himself, Christy would have been struggling to get her boots on by herself when he'd walked into the classroom.

Kelly twisted in her seat in time to see his smug smile. "I saw that."

Chuckling, Chad said, "You sound just like my fourth-grade teacher. That's what she said after a spitball bounced off the blackboard."

One you undoubtedly flicked, she thought. Teachers didn't have eyes in the back of their heads, but they instinctively knew who the culprits were. Usually it was the child looking wide-eyed and innocent.

Realizing she'd prejudged him for no real reason, Kelly suddenly felt guilty and knew her face was turning red.

She wasn't the only one in the car feeling guilty. Chad's smile hid a sharp pang of regret. He'd deliberately tried to trick her by making it seem as if helping Christy with her boots was robbing the child of self-reliance. He wasn't proud of his attempt at one-upmanship.

"Forget it." A thin haze of fog coated the inside of the windshield. Chad switched on the defrosters and swiped at the glass. Driving slowly to avoid going into a skid, he turned into the store's parking lot. Leaving the engine running to keep Kelly warm, he said, "Hold on to Tiger. I'll get the dog food."

He was out of the car and gone before Kelly could protest. He'd been kind enough to drive her to the store; she should have been the one slipping and sliding across the parking lot. She hadn't even given him any money.

Wiggles's wet nose nuzzled between her breasts, seeking warmth as she shifted the strap of her purse off her shoulder. "You're okay, Wiggles," she said soothingly, feeling less than okay herself.

She hadn't the vaguest idea how much a bag of dog food cost. Five dollars? Ten? She unsnapped her billfold. Better to overpay than be in debt, she decided.

A look of dismay crossed her face. Darn it, she'd cashed a check yesterday. Where was the money? Mentally backtracking, she remembered taking the cash out her purse and putting it in the cabinet over the kitchen sink. She trusted her students, but there wasn't any reason to tempt them by carelessly leaving money in her purse.

Maybe I've got enough change, she thought as she opened the compartment that held coins.

"Terrific," she groaned sarcastically. "A dime and a quarter."

She shook her purse hoping for the rattle of loose silver, but she heard only the sound of Wiggles's soft whimper at being disturbed by the shaking.

"Great! How do you feel about washing doggy dishes, Mr. Wiggles?"

The puppy responded by licking her. His stubby tail swished against her waist.

"None of that," she said, hugging the puppy and grinning. "Kisses won't pay for dog food."

She stuck her billfold back in her purse and sighed. Then a wicked thought crossed her mind. Wouldn't Uncle Charming be shocked if Christy's teacher paid him for the dog food with a big kiss? Of course, she wouldn't do anything so outrageous, but the fleeting thought made her laugh nervously.

She shook her head to stop her flight into fantasy. Even the slowest underachiever would have been astute enough to tell her she had the story backward. Kissing Prince Charming wouldn't change her into a princess with a Florida suntan.

"No, Mr. Wiggles, we won't be impractical. While Chad waits in the car, I'll carry you and the dog food into the house, then I'll take the money from the cabinet and pay him."

While Kelly was rehearsing for a polite handshake and a gracious thank-you, Chad was lugging five pounds of Puppy Chow, a chewy bone and a flea collar toward the checkout counter. He wondered for the hundredth time why he was going so far out of his way to help Kelly. What was it about her that affected him so?

From the instant he'd first glanced at her, the tug on his heartstrings had been impossible to ignore. As he'd watched her struggle to put on Christy's boots, an inner voice had told him that years ago, when he'd been a child, the scenario would have ended with a severe scolding from any elementary school teacher he'd had. But instead of bawling Christy out, Kelly had laughed.

Was it her compassion or her laughter that had caused goose bumps to rise on his arms?

When she'd refused his offer of a ride home because she had to tutor a student who had been absent, his admiration had grown. By Friday afternoon, most of the teachers he'd known could have qualified for the Indianapolis 500 in their rush to beat the buses out of the parking lot. Frankly, he admired anyone who devoted extra time and energy to his job—especially a teacher.

Compassion, dedication and a sense of humor, he mused as he tossed a box of animal crackers in the cart. Those were traits he looked for in his business associates but not necessarily in the women he dated.

A wry smile crossed his lips. Who said anything about dating her? At the rate things were going, he'd be lucky if she continued to speak to him.

Perseverance, he thought. He'd learned it at an early age. No obstacle was too difficult to be overcome. There had been occasions when he'd been frustrated, when he'd felt like giving up. But, despite being subject to "burning kissability" he'd had enough gumption to know the only limitations holding him back were the limits he placed on himself. While others had been perfecting the three R's, he'd learned how to dream. For years his dreams had been the only thing that kept him from being a loser. He'd dared to be different, unique. Except for a brief period in his midtwenties, when he'd put his parent's priorities ahead of his own, he'd always been his own man.

He realized that by most people's standards he still must seem a little odd. Researching foreign patents, contacting the patentholders and negotiating rights to produce and market those inventions in the United States was considered extremely risky by conservative businessmen.

Chad couldn't care less about other people's financial hang-ups regarding having a monthly paycheck. If he lost the shirt off his back, he'd dream up a way to get a new one. Being independent had advantages that far outweighed the drawbacks. Had he been stuck behind a desk, he wouldn't have been able to leave Florida on a moment's notice to help with his sister's children. When his brother-in-law had called to tell him his sister was about to have her new baby, he'd packed several boxes of paperwork and flown to St. Louis.

Grinning, he tacked on another fringe benefit to being self-employed. Had he been shackled to a regular job, he wouldn't have met Miz Mallory.

He stopped at the checkout counter, selected an array of candy bars and handed them to the cashier along with the contents of the cart. Half listening, nodding whenever the cashier spoke, he began to formulate a plan.

Minutes later, Chad grinned as he opened the car door. He saw the questioning look on Kelly's face as he put two large sacks on the back seat. He'd made it through two decades of schooling with the undisputed title of class clown thanks to his bottomless bag of tricks, and he hadn't grown rusty since graduation. Surely the items in the second bag would keep Miz Mallory amused for the evening...and maybe longer.

Three

───────

Thanks for the ride and for getting the puppy food."
Kelly started her canned spiel the moment the front
wheels touched her driveway. As Chad put the car in
park and reached for the keys, she began talking so
quickly she was nearly babbling. "Just leave the engine running. I'll be back in a flash with the money to
pay for the groceries. Don't bother getting out into the
bad weather again."

"No bother." He grinned and switched off the ig-
nition. "I wouldn't think of bringing you this far, then
sitting in the car while you made faceprints in the
snow. Stay put. I'll get you inside first. Then I'll come
back for the groceries."

"You stay put.... I'll be right back. I insist."

"Nope. I insist. What would Christy think of her uncle if he drove her favorite teacher home and dumped her in the driveway. You wouldn't want to destroy my reputation, would you?"

"Of course not, but—" She stopped herself from promising not to tell on him. "I can manage," she assured him weakly.

"I don't doubt you're self-reliant. Think of my helping you as a form of repayment for your helping Christy with her boots."

"That's my...job." Further protest was impossible. She was talking to thin air. Chad was out of the car and circling the front fender. "Darn it, Wiggles. See what you and Christy have gotten me into!"

Hearing his name, Wiggles peered out of the warm cocoon he'd made. Ears raised, he cocked his head to one side and wagged his tail. His paws kneaded her breasts as he clamored to get free.

"Oh, no, you don't, mister. You're staying right where you are until you're inside. Don't you want some puppy food?"

Holding greased lightning would have been easier. The moment the door opened, Wiggles jumped, landing with a soft splat in the fresh snow. With a surprised look and a mighty shake, he burrowed into the drift. Before he could backtrack and escape, Chad scooped him up with one hand.

"Come on, Trouble," Chad said, unbuttoning his coat and dropping him inside. Feeling the little dog's icy paws against his shirtfront, Chad shivered involuntarily.

Kelly took the hand he extended to her. Through her woolen mitten she shouldn't have been able to feel the warmth of his skin, but she could. Perhaps it was her imagination playing tricks on her.

"Lean on me," Chad instructed, and wrapped his arm around her shoulder.

What could she do? To keep her balance she had to put her arm around his waist, didn't she? Several layers of clothing should have protected her from feeling the power of his arm, back and thigh, but they didn't. *My heart shouldn't accelerate like this just because he's literally taken me under his protective wing,* Kelly told herself. *Where is all that self-reliance I spouted off about?*

Drowning in the sweaty palm of your hand, she told herself dejectedly. She couldn't have been more physically aware of him if they'd both been wearing skimpy swimsuits while strolling a moonlit Florida beach.

She glanced upward. Snowflakes clung to Chad's blond hair. His deep tan contrasted with the whiteness of the snow, reminding her that Chad Turner preferred a warmer climate. He wouldn't be in St. Louis for any length of time.

"Key?"

Caught staring up at him, Kelly made a production of finding her keys in the bottom of her purse. As he opened the storm door, she shifted beneath his arm to insert the key into the lock. Her shaking hand spoiled her aim, and she missed. Annoyed by being unable to perform even this simple task, she jabbed the key forward and somehow managed to miss again.

"Is the lock frozen?"

He leaned forward over her shoulder and gave her nose an unexpected treat. Sunshine, she thought, recognizing the smell. Someone has bottled sunshine commercially? Knowing that was impossible, she sniffed to make certain. Definitely sunshine.

"You're freezing. Your hand is shaking." He closed his hand over hers and took the key. Realizing she'd been trying to put the key in upside-down brought a smile to his lips. It was nice to know being close to him was having a debilitating effect on her self-sufficiency. He easily unlocked the door.

Kelly flipped on all three switches in the foyer. Out of nervousness, she quoted a nursery rhyme, saying, "Home again, home again, jiggity-jog." As soon as she shut her mouth again, she felt perfectly inane.

He looked around the lit area. The living room had the same colors as those contained in a box of eight crayons. There were no pastels, only bold, bright colors. White leather furniture begged to be sprawled on. Modernistic drawings were mounted on clear blue, green, yellow, red and purple matboard. Accent pieces and handcrafted pottery balanced the color scheme.

He liked what he saw.

"Here you go, Pooch. You check this place out while I get your food." To Kelly he added, "Be back in a second."

"That's what I'm afraid of," she muttered as she closed the door behind him. "What am I going to do with him?"

Wiggles sniffed twice, shook, then tramped into the adjoining room.

Unable to find an answer to her question, she watched the puppy. He was making himself right at home—on the cream-colored carpet.

"Wiggles! No!" Todd had promised the puppy was paper-trained. There wasn't a scrap of paper anywhere to be seen.

With a what-am-I-doing-wrong expression, Wiggles cowered over the small damp spot he'd made.

Pulling a Kleenex from her coat pocket, she dabbed at the carpet. Something struck her as being wrong. Male dogs didn't squat. Wiggles had.

"Are you sure your name is Mister Wiggles?" She picked him up, checked out his anatomy and sighed. He was a male dog, but obviously he was too young to know it. "That's not where...or how you do it. Haven't you heard about trees, bushes and fire hydrants? The great out-of-doors?" She paused. The puppy looked at her uncomprehendingly. "You say it's too cold?"

Kelly groaned as she realized she was not only talking to the dog, she was answering. "I suppose it's only natural that I should be going crazy. It's been a crazy day."

Marching into the kitchen, she opened the pantry, pulled out a stack of papers and took them to the laundry room. "This is where. I don't know what we're going to do about how." Grinning wryly as she unfolded the sheets, she added, "There are some subjects I'm not qualified to teach."

She put Wiggles down. "Well?"

Wiggles sniffed the paper and gave her a wary glance.

"I don't expect you to read it," she chided good-naturedly. She removed her coat and scarf, tossing them on the washer, then sat down beside the obviously perplexed puppy.

Wiggles sat down, too. His pink tongue lolled out the side of his mouth. His bottom wiggled on the paper as his tail swished back and forth on the newsprint.

Her heart went out to him. He was so ugly that he was adorable. Without a doubt he was the most all-American dog she'd ever seen, a melting pot of every breed known to man. His huge, floppy ears and tail didn't belong with his stubby legs and compact body. His pug nose was too small for the large eyes above it. Although mostly white, he had a liberal sprinkling of irregular black and brown spots. It was as though his genes had seen the puppy, felt sorry for him and at the last possible moment used a pepper shaker to try to make him more appealing. All in all, the most dignified part of the puppy was the name Todd had given him.

The name Chad refused to utter.

"Kelly?" Chad called from the doorway.

At least he's got *my* name right, she thought. "I'm in the laundry room. Mr. Wiggles has a little problem."

Following the sound of her voice, Chad crossed into the kitchen, set the grocery bags on a counter, shed his coat and moved to the laundry room doorway.

"Anything I can help with?" he offered.

"How much do you know about potty-training a dog?"

Chad grinned. "Kids get potty-trained. Dogs go outside."

"Smart aleck." With a final pat of encouragement on Wiggles's head, she rose, keeping a vigilant eye on the puppy. "You knew what I meant."

Chad's grin widened. His blue eyes twinkled with suppressed laughter as he noticed the paw prints on her blouse. Oh, for a dog's life, he thought.

Only inches away from Chad, she felt as if the room was closing in on her. "What do I do now?"

Several suggestions came to Chad's mind, but he stifled them and cleared his throat. As certain as he was that she'd be too soft-hearted to spank the puppy for having an accident on the carpet, he also felt certain she wouldn't take kindly to his suggesting that she take off her blouse.

"He needs a bed," Chad suggested. His voice sounded strained. "Something with your scent on it will make him feel secure. Something out of that basket should do."

"Makes sense." Her face flamed when she glanced at the clothes in the basket. Right on top was the load of lingerie she'd planned on washing by hand. Lacy bras, teddies, slips and panties comprised the frothy pile. "Uh, it's a bit crowded in here."

Unable to resist teasing her, he picked up a coffee-colored teddy edged with cream lace. "I thought teachers wore starched underwear and taffeta petticoats...nothing sexy."

Kelly bit her tongue to keep from shouting, "Give that to me this instant!" Uh-uh, she thought, and took a deep breath to steady her nerves.

"You must be Christy's great-great-great-uncle. Dress codes went out years ago," she replied, indifferently as she could. She forced her eyes away from his hand, which still held the Chantilly lace fringe, and looked at the granny nightgown in the bottom of the basket. "This should do," she said picking up the nightgown.

"Flannel at night and peek-a-boo lace during the day." His brown eyes sparkled mischievously. "Wonder what the school psychologist would say about that?"

Kelly fussed with the nightgown's fabric. Keeping her fingers busy helped to ease the tension, but part of her wanted to wrap the nightgown around Chad's neck and pull very tightly.

"Probably the same thing he said when I took several crayon pictures done by one of my students for him to analyse." She knelt on the newspaper, picked Wiggles up and deposited him in the cozy bed she'd made. "The child seemed perfectly normal—bright, well-adjusted, happy—until art class. Her pictures were always done in brown, purple, grey and black."

"What did the shrink say?"

Kelly grinned. "He suggested I move her to the front of the room."

"So she'd get more attention?"

"Uh-uh. So she'd get first pick from the box of crayons I passed around. Seated in the back of the room, she had to choose the dark colors because they were the only ones left." Fingering the flannel, she added, "I bought this nightgown on sale. There weren't any others left that fit into my budget."

Chuckling, Chad offered his hand to help her to her feet. "What kind of nightgowns do you prefer?"

Deciding it was the appropriate time to bring this conversation to a halt, she replied. "Ones that fit my budget. Speaking of expenses, how much do I owe you for the dog food?"

She thought she'd won the verbal skirmish until she felt his fingers curl around her hand. One seemingly effortless yank on his part propelled her off the floor and into his arms.

"Nothing. Now for the big, revealing question," he whispered, tilting her chin upward with his thumb. "If you had an unlimited budget, would you wear sexy nightgowns?"

Pressed against him from shoulder to thigh, she couldn't say anything—especially about what she'd wear to bed. The fragrance of sunshine and the warmth emanating from him made her feel as though the sun had swallowed her whole. Like Icarus, who made wings of wax and flew too close to the sun, she felt as if her bones were melting against him. Her mouth was parched, and her heart was doing silly flip-flops. A thin thread of rationality told her it was impossible on a snowy November night to have sunstroke, but she certainly had all the symptoms.

Chad had expected her to be rigid, unyielding in his arms. Her soft pliancy surprised him and ignited a flash fire he couldn't control. He was the one who was suddenly uptight and nervous.

Back at the store, he'd planned on being her class clown, but he hadn't planned on making a fool of himself.

Uncertain of what he'd do if she replied to his provocative question, he released her, turned and strode into the kitchen.

Kelly braced her hand on the washing machine to keep from dropping to her knees. It didn't take a chemistry major to define the reaction touching him had on her: spontaneous combustion.

Inhaling deeply in an effort to steady the rapid beating of her heart, she wondered why he'd walked away. Her experience was limited, but there was no mistaking his reaction. He'd wanted to kiss her. She'd seen desire flare in his eyes. He couldn't have misread the signals her body was sending, either.

Why? she wondered. Why had he turned his back on her?

Unwillingly she admitted to herself that she couldn't have moved away from him if her life had depended upon it. Quite the contrary. Had he held her a moment longer, she would have been unable to stop her arms from encircling his neck, her fingers from touching his hair, or her lips from closing over his.

Why had she felt so safe when he'd held her close to him? She should have panicked. She couldn't explain her own reactions rationally.

This breath-stealing, heart-racing, mind-blowing assault Chad Turner had made on her senses wasn't what she wanted. She was too sensible, too practical, too smart to let mere physical attraction knock her for a loop.

She glanced down at Mr. Wiggles. Exhausted from his frolic in the snow, he'd snuggled into the folds of her nightgown and fallen asleep. Some protector you are, she thought. Any other red-blooded watchdog would at least have snarled when an intruder grabbed his master.

She looked at the entryway to the kitchen when she heard the sound of rustling paper, footsteps, then the creaking of the oven door being opened. What was he doing? Broiling the dog's food? She'd heard of eccentric rich people preparing gourmet dishes for their dogs, but Chad struck her as the type who couldn't boil water without scorching the pan.

"What are you cooking?" she asked from the doorway.

"Pizza. Pepperoni for me. Sausage for you. Or vice versa."

"We're dining together? Here?" she asked.

"Any objections?"

"Hundreds...thousands!" she sputtered.

"Such as?"

"Don't you think you're being a bit presumptuous?"

"Not really. I figure any woman who'd carry a puppy two miles through knee-deep snow was too softhearted to send the man who rescued her back out into the blizzard without feeding him first. Especially when I provide the dinner and cook it." He paused, turned and shot her a winning smile. "Right?"

Kelly rubbed her forehead in consternation. Bulldozer tactics, she thought. "You don't happen to know my brother, Tom Mallory, do you?"

"No. Why? Are you expecting him for dinner?"

"Uh-uh, but I think I'm about to eat dinner with his blond-headed twin."

Taking that as a good sign, Chad asked hopefully, "Your favorite brother?"

"Hardly. Dad used to threaten to lock both of us in a closet until we learned to get along with each other. Out of three older brothers and two younger sisters, Tom was the only one I could have cheerfully throttled."

"The proverbial black sheep," Chad said, feeling deflated by her reply.

"Coal-black," Kelly readily agreed. "But I'm the only woman who isn't color-blind when he walks into a room. The rest of the world's female population sees him as a modern version of Casanova the lover."

"He must have some saving grace they see."

"Just charm."

Their eyes met. *Uncle Charming,* Christy's nickname for Chad rang between them in the silence.

Briefly Chad wondered if Shannon considered him a black sheep. She wouldn't, he decided. He and his sister were much alike, double trouble with a genetic link.

Wondering about this brother, who Kelly seemed to think was so much like him, he asked, "Do your brothers get along with him?"

Kelly chuckled in spite of herself. "Oh, yes. He's a man's man. Pete and Greg would trade places with him in a minute. Not only is he blessed with good looks and charm, Tom is the luckiest person alive. For example—" Kelly crossed to the dinette chair and sat down "—three years ago he talked me into being fixed up with his girlfriend's brother. We went across the river to the horse races in East St. Louis. By the third race, he was down to his last dollar."

"That's lucky?"

"Purely a mistake on Lady Luck's part, believe me," she replied dryly. "To give the devil his due, I have to admit that Tom did refuse money from his girlfriend and her brother. His little-boy-lost look even made me take pity on him, but he wouldn't take money from me, either. Anyway, to make a long story short, on his way to get refreshments for the rest of us he used his last dollar to buy a lottery ticket. Guess what?"

"He was an instant winner?"

"Bingo! He collected a hundred dollars. He went directly to the ticket window and bet it on a long shot. Two hours later he walked away with a wad of bills big enough to choke a racehorse." Smoothing her slacks over her knees, she added, "I'd lay odds that you're lucky, too, aren't you?"

Chad wanted to deny her accusation, but he couldn't lie. He'd made quite a lot of money in his thirty-two years, and he had to admit that some of it had been due to luck. Besides, being at the right place at the right time had brought him to her doorstep, hadn't it?

"Yeah," he admitted as he shoved his hands into his pockets. Slowly he approached her. "I wouldn't be here now if I weren't lucky. A blizzard, my sister and niece and a puppy were Lady Luck's tools. Without luck I'd be pacing the floor at my sister's house cursing the weather instead of talking to the sexiest teacher in St. Louis."

Kelly smiled weakly. Luck, charm and persistence were a tough combination to resist. Like her brother, Chad was a born winner.

The oven's timer buzzed.

Chad asked, "Would I be pushing my luck if I took the pizzas from the oven and shared them with you?"

"Yes." Her smiled widened into a grin when she recognized the obstinate glint in his eyes. "But that isn't going to stop you, is it?"

Chad winked, then swaggered to the stove and turned off the buzzer. "Contrary to popular belief, good luck does rub off. I wouldn't want you to miss an opportunity to have some of mine rub off on you. Who knows, if you get really lucky, it might even rub some of those paw prints off your blouse."

Halfway to her feet to get something for them to drink, Kelly plopped back in the chair. For the first time, she saw the dark smudges that made a path from one breast to the other. Thoughts of Chad staring at that path brought a pink blush to her cheeks.

Chad couldn't restrain a hoot of laughter, and Kelly leaped to her feet. She squelched the urge to flounce into the bedroom, slam the door and lock it behind her.

Kelly's eyes narrowed. She was determined not to let him see how embarrassed she was. Fingers splayed, she ran her hands from her rib cage down to her hips. Doing her best Mae West imitation, she said, "Stick around, big boy. I'll be right back to help you with your... homework."

Satisfaction brought a smug smile to her lips when she saw the look of astonishment on his face. With an exaggerated, slinky sway of her hips, she walked toward the hallway leading to the bedroom.

"Touché!" Chad muttered as she disappeared.

Kelly clamped her hand over her mouth after she'd closed the bedroom door. He'd gotten the last word, but it was an accolade—something she'd never expected.

She removed the blouse and she darted to the dresser. Feeling victorious, she found herself speculating on what Chad's reaction would be if she reappeared braless, wearing a clingy sweater. For a moment she actually considered doing it—actually wanted to do it. Then certain she must be losing her slender grasp on reality she pulled a lilac sweater from the bottom drawer and put it on. As the sweater slid over her head, Kelly reaffirmed her resolve to be calm, cool and collected—no matter what effect Chad had on her emotional thermostat.

She shoved the sleeves up to her elbows, but just as she picked up the brush to take care of her mussed hair she heard Chad shout from the kitchen.

"Pizza's getting cold."

He glanced at his watch. It had taken him a good five minutes to recover from Kelly's exit. At first he'd been floored by her swinging hips and saucy words. By the time he'd fanned his face, set the table and opened Cokes he'd realized she'd played the role of seductress to perfection.

But that was what it was for her, he was certain: a role. She'd been acting, pretending, setting his imagination on fire, but she had no intention of going any further.

He cocked his head toward the closed bedroom door, but couldn't hear anything. Had his innocent temptress had a change of heart? Had she locked herself in the bathroom to avoid confronting him?

"Kelly?"

"I'm coming."

Chad breathed a sigh of relief. For a moment he'd thought he'd pushed his luck too far. Reaching into his bag of tricks, he grabbed a box of animal crackers. As she rounded the corner, he tossed them to her.

"Good catch," he said, grinning, and examining her from head to foot. Huggable, he decided, taking notice of how soft and delicate she appeared. Believing that women who look huggable should be hugged, he closed the space between them. "This must be your lucky day, too."

Four

———

Animal crackers and a hug?''

Without knowing why, Kelly realized both pleased her enormously. She couldn't remember a time when anyone, apart from her mother, had fixed dinner for her. Usually when she invited someone for a meal, she was doing it to vanquish guilty feelings over something she'd done. As she sat down, she tilted her head to one side, wondering if this was Chad's way of apologizing for yelling at her after she'd dived in front of his car to save Wiggles from being injured.

While he efficiently sliced both pizzas, she wondered if she'd misjudged him. A Florida tan didn't necessarily mean he was a playboy. People did go to Florida to work, didn't they?

"So," she began, determined to find out if Chad was among the ranks of the unemployed, "what do you do for a living that lets you winter in Florida?"

Here it comes, Chad mused, none to happy with the question. Was she trying to pigeonhole him, or was she just on the lookout for a well-to-do man? Why was it that when a woman wanted to know how successful a man was, she asked where he worked? Men used the same economic barometer, but coming from a woman, that question seemed to be a veiled way of asking, "Can you support me in the manner I'd like to become accustomed to?"

Chad refrained from correcting her mistaken assumption that he led a vagabond existence. He refused to try to prove himself worthy by meeting another person's standards, especially a woman's. He'd met his share of money-hungry females, and although Kelly didn't seem to be one of them, there was no way to tell for sure. The very look in her eyes when she'd asked what he did for a living disturbed him. No, Chad thought, for the time being she'd have to take him or leave him at face value.

Deliberately being evasive, he replied, "Oh, a little of this and a little of that."

"This and that . . . what?"

Chad grinned. "Whatever *this* and *that* strikes me as being fun."

Barely managing to stifle a groan, Kelly pulled a wedge of pizza from the tray. His unsatisfactory reply was as irritating as the string of cheese still connecting her piece of pizza to the tray. Kelly scissored the cheese between her fingers, took a bite of the pie and chewed.

He did whatever he thought was fun, she mused. Fun—that was a word she'd often used in the classroom: Reading is fun. Learning is fun. Fun with numbers. During her first year as a teacher, she'd discovered that games were the best tool for teaching skills. She devoted considerable time and effort to making learning fun.

Then why was she disgruntled with his reply? Logically she shouldn't find fault with Chad's wanting his work to be fun. And yet she did.

As though Chad had invaded her mind and known exactly what she was thinking, he asked, "Is teaching fun?"

"Most of the time, yes."

"What do you like the best?"

"The look on children's faces when they've caught on to a new idea. They light up like a Christmas tree."

"And the least?"

Kelly had to think for a minute. "Being a mini-banker. Collecting for lunches, pictures, insurance, parties, etcetera, etcetera. That's something teacher education courses delete...otherwise we'd be required to take accounting classes." She raised her eyebrow. "Are you considering entering the teaching profession?"

Laughing, Chad wiped some tomato sauce from his mouth with a paper napkin. "Heavens, no. School and marriage are institutions I've purposely avoided. What about you? Why aren't you married?"

Kelly had the same sinking sensation in her stomach she felt when she carefully planned a lesson only to have the kids divert her attention to a subject she wanted to avoid. Discussing her reasons for not being married ranked right up there with listening to a first-grader rehash the latest blood-and-guts television program during show-and-tell.

She swiped at an imaginary crumb on her lap and considered dodging his question. Reluctantly she rejected the idea, but decided that if he mentioned anything about old-maid schoolteachers she'd kick him out the front door.

"I haven't been asked."

Rocking back in his chair, Chad studied her. "Why?"

"Lots of reasons, according to the women's magazines. Women outnumber men. Women are too choosy, too educated, too independent. The reasons go on and on."

Wanting to escape from his steady stare, she rose, gathered her pizza tray and dumped it into the garbage.

The front legs of the chair thudded to the floor as he straightened and began to clean up his mess. "I don't read women's magazines. Personally, I'm beginning to wonder if all the men in St. Louis are going blind and I haven't heard about it on the national news."

Amused by his compliment, Kelly chuckled. "I haven't read about increased enrollment at the St. Louis Institute for the Blind. But, come to think of it, one of the magazine articles did say that the ratio between single men and women is higher in the Sun Belt. Maybe all the eligible men are doing what you do for a living...searching for fun, making footprints in the sand and watching them being swept out to sea." She pulled a scoop from a drawer and opened the freezer. "This is an equal opportunity kitchen. You fixed dinner; I'll fix dessert. Vanilla or rocky road?"

"Rocky road." He pointed to the cabinet to the left of the sink. "Bowls in there?"

Kelly nodded.

Seeing the scowl on his face, Kelly wondered if he hated both flavors she'd offered. Automatically an apology formed on the tip of her tongue. She swallowed it. Sausage pizza wasn't her favorite, but she'd eaten it.

"Potluck," she muttered, scooping two dips of rocky road into the bowl he held in his hand. "Potluck means you take what's available and pretend it's your favorite."

A devilish light entered his brown eyes. "Like taking a puppy you didn't choose and risking your life to save it? Or wearing flannel when you want lace?" Chad turned his back and strolled to the table. "Tell me, Kelly, would you take any available man and pretend he's your favorite?"

Dropping a scoop of vanilla ice cream into her bowl, Kelly seriously considered heaving the ice cream, bowl and scoop at Chad. Calm, cool and collected, she reminded herself as she placed the container in the freezer and rinsed the scoop.

A mental picture of Phillip entered her mind. Phillip was available. She had tried to convince Trudy that Phillip was the right kind of man for her. Inwardly she cringed. Was she willing to settle for potluck love? Leftovers? Hand-me-downs?

She turned off the tap, dried her hands, picked up the ice cream bowl and followed Chad. Smarting from two people implying that she was a certifiable chump in one day, she seated herself and glared at the smug smile on his face. "No," she finally answered, as casually as if they were still talking about ice cream.

"Good." He opened the box of animal crackers and selected a monkey with a lopsided smile and handed it to her. "I'm not interested in potluck relationships, either."

"You mean you're assuming you and I are going to have some type of relationship?"

"Definitely."

Chad ate his ice cream eagerly while Kelly's melted in her bowl.

"Your conceit surpasses my selflessness," she quipped, smiling before biting off the monkey's head and wondering how she was going to survive this evening.

"Impossible. You're a born giver. I had to learn self-confidence the hard way." He licked the residue of ice cream from his spoon, thoroughly enjoying the irritation he'd heard in her voice. He hadn't lost his touch; he could still get the teacher's attention with his brashness. Sure that no man had managed to ruffle her feathers so thoroughly, he added, "Like it or not, I'm going to put some fun in your life, teach."

With that proclamation he took his empty bowl to the sink, turned, picked up his coat and strode toward the front door.

"Wait a minute." Kelly jumped to her feet and rushed after him. "You're leaving?"

He buttoned his coat and raised the collar to ward off the biting wind. "Are you offering to let me spend the night?" he asked audaciously.

"Of course not, but—"

"Pity." He faked a deep sigh and brushed the back of his knuckles along her cheek. "Lovemaking could be your first lesson in Fun 101."

Kelly's face flamed. She grabbed the doorknob, twisted it and flung the door wide open. "You've missed the prerequisites for Fun 101, such as Respect, Admiration and Friendship 100. Good night, Mr. Turner."

Undaunted by her sudden lack of hospitality, Chad called over her shoulder, "G'night." Then, after a slight hesitation, he turned, pulled Kelly into his arms and dropped a light kiss on her parted lips. "See you."

Wanting to rob her of the satisfaction of slamming the door in his face, Chad closed it himself. Although he was dead certain she was fuming, he chuckled when the front porch light came on. She's slow to provoke, quick to respond, unable to hold a grudge and always wants to please, he deduced. And she loves to have the final word.

"Not this time, Miz Mallory," he promised quietly as he spied a snow shovel beside the front steps. Actions speak louder than words, he thought. Carefully moving from the porch to the sidewalk, he picked up the shovel and began scooping mounds of snow off the steps.

Kelly pressed her ear against the door when she heard a strange scraping sound. He's shoveling my walk! she thought. Here I've practically tossed him out of the house and he's doing me a favor? Why hadn't he jumped in his car and backtracked out of her life as quickly as he'd entered it? That was what she wanted, not this continuing feeling of being beholden to him.

Tempted to pull the door open and tell him she was perfectly capable of clearing the snow from her sidewalk, she gripped the doorknob, but in an instant she felt a sharp pang of guilt and uncurled her fingers. Yelling at a man for being nice wasn't fair.

"Fair? Chad Turner doesn't know the first thing about fighting *fair*," she muttered, folding her arms over her chest.

Her brothers and sisters knew how to fight fair. Their style was knock-down-and-drag-out fights followed by killing silences, and wariness. Then Kelly the peacemaker would have to negotiate an agreeable settlement. Rarely could they get her to participate during the heat of battle. She avoided confrontations, but during the few short hours she'd been with Chad, her blood pressure must have risen ten points. She'd come closer than ever before to waging all-out war, and with an unscrupulous man who fought dirty.

She raised her fingers to her mouth. Kissing an angry woman was fighting dirty, wasn't it? Reflexively her tongue ran over her bottom lip. On the spot where he'd lightly kissed her, a hint of sunshine lingered. Ridiculous! A person could feel sunshine, smell sunshine, see sunshine, but it didn't have a flavor.

Pondering the possibility, she slowly crossed to the living room's bay window.

Kelly gave the cord on the draperies a hefty yank. She wouldn't let him intimidate her into peeking through the slit to avoid being seen. Feet apart, hands on her hips, she watched him make short work of the snow on the porch and progress down the sidewalk.

His movements were smooth, fluid. He handled the shovel as though he'd been born with one in his hand. What would have been almost impossible for her, he accomplished with ease.

Her eyes widened with concern when she noticed he wasn't wearing gloves. Although she almost thought he deserved any blisters that might result from his work, she really didn't want him to hurt himself shoveling her walk. She waved her arms to get his attention.

Glancing toward the house as he shoveled, Chad saw Kelly's frantic attempt to get his attention. She pointed at her hand, then at him. One hand motioned in small circles, indicating that he should come back inside.

Chad grinned, shook his head and returned to his chore. Scooping up shovelfuls of snow had the same effect as a cold shower. Little did Kelly realize how much he wanted to accept her entreaty. Offhand he could think of a dozen wonderful ways she could warm his hands. The only problem was that other parts of his body would get hot as well.

The fantasy of lazily making love to Kelly had been lurking in the back of his mind. Suddenly it jumped forward, jarring through him. He wanted Kelly Mallory. He began to shovel faster than he thought was possible.

From the moment he'd casually touched her and felt an electrical charge that threatened to curl his hair, he'd wanted more of her. The brief moment he'd held her in his arms and kissed her had merely whetted his appetite. In a way, his parting kiss had been a test to see what shock tactics were necessary to break down Kelly's ample defenses. What would it take to get her to come to him willingly? To feel her arms twine around him, to make her beg for his kisses?

"Too soon," he whispered breathily.

Confident she wasn't the sort of woman who even kissed on the first encounter, he contented himself with knowing he'd left a lasting impression on her. He wouldn't have to nearly run her down in the middle of the street to get her attention anymore. No, he mused, glancing toward her house. This was one teacher who was going to give him her undivided attention.

Kelly parked in the assigned space next to Trudy's car. While gathering the papers she'd graded over the weekend with one hand, she pulled her knitted cap farther down on her forehead with the other.

St. Louis remained locked in the icy grips of another Arctic blast. Glancing through the windshield at the low-hanging snow clouds, Kelly prayed for a break in the weather.

"A little sunshine, Lord. That's not too much to ask, is it?"

When she heard a rhythmic knock on the window she glanced to the left, and her heart lurched. She'd asked for sunshine. Why was she so shocked to see Mr. Sunshine himself outside her door, grinning at her.

"Good morning," he said, opening her door. "Let me carry those books and papers for you."

The look Kelly shot him was even colder than the air in St. Louis that day. Sidestepping him, her belongings held tightly against her coat front, she walked briskly toward the building.

Why shouldn't she be cool toward him? She'd wasted the entire weekend thinking up clever remarks to make when he unexpectedly appeared on her doorstep. There had been only one problem. He hadn't shown up. She had to admit that fact had disturbed her much more than it should have. She thought the very least he could have done was call and inquire about Mr. Wiggles. For all he knew, she could have been bottle-feeding him dinosaur juice.

At midnight on Saturday she had tossed and turned in her bed, vowing never again to hang her pillow outside to capture the fragrance of the sun. If someone had been in the room with her, they'd have sworn she was coming down with some rare tropical disease.

She'd sniffed her pillow dozens of times to see if a hint of sunshine remained buried inside the feathers.

Sunday she'd graded papers and planned a science experiment. When thoughts of Chad Turner had tried to sneak into her mind, she'd squelched them by eating the two boxes of animal crackers he'd bought. That evening she'd convinced herself that her imagination must have been in overdrive Friday night. His looks and all the things he'd said were simply part of his charm, she tried to tell herself. He'd said them so often that he sounded convincing even when he was insincere. She'd been naive to believe his compliments were anything other than charming lies. And lies were lies.

Chad rushed after her. "I drove Christy to school."

"That's nice," she said in her most civil tone, so angry she even forgot to ask how Shannon was. *Get out of my face, Uncle Charming* was what she wanted to reply.

She stuck her hand into her large coat pocket as she kept her eyes straight ahead and marched toward the school. Maddeningly, he walked so close behind her that she couldn't avoid smelling his sunshine fragrance.

Chad felt unaccountably annoyed. Kelly was giving him the same get-lost-I'm-busy routine he'd gotten in elementary school. He'd race to school, eager to talk with his teacher, and she'd give him the brush-off with some weak excuse like "Sit down, Chad. I'm taking attendance." It was just another defense he realized. Kelly was acting more like the perfect teacher than a real woman. It was easier and safer for her to do so, he knew. But that didn't matter. Eventually he'd get behind the defenses, destroy the perfect-teacher person and find the flesh-and-blood woman beneath it.

As he walked behind her, he noticed her shivering, and that gave him an idea. "I've made arrangements for you to go to Florida with me during Thanksgiving vacation," he announced.

That stopped her.

She wheeled around, blue eyes flashing. "You've what?"

Chad grinned. That got her attention, he thought. It certainly worked better than presenting this teacher with a shiny red apple.

"Good idea, huh?" He wrapped his arm around her shoulders and gave her a hug.

Kelly quickly pulled free of his loose grip. "I'm not going to Florida or anywhere else with you. I barely know you."

"Exactly. That's why it's such a great idea. What better way to get to know each other?"

Yeah, Kelly thought. You mean get to know each other in the biblical sense. She glanced upward to see if a masculine leer curved his lips. He was smiling, but not really leering. Pleased with himself, she deduced. His invitation was spontaneous, she realized, not part of some master plan he'd been working on to seduce her. In a way, he reminded her of some of the mischievous but lovable boys in her class.

But Chad isn't a child, she silently reminded herself. He's an attractive man and you're a . . . spinster?

God, she hated that word—almost as much as she hated the idea of traipsing off to Florida with a man who was little more than a stranger.

Chad tried to interpret her glance and the silence that followed. Was that a good sign or a bad one? At least her steps had slowed. She wasn't racing into the building to get away from him.

He leaned down to her ear and said huskily, "The past two days I've thought a lot about you."

"I'll bet," she snapped peevishly.

"You'd lose." He caught her elbow to stop her. "I thought of you constantly. I wanted to be with you, but each time I got within ten feet of the telephone I had a minor crisis on my hands. I swear, Shannon's kids are pint-size demolition experts on twenty-four-hour call."

Believing him without question, Kelly grinned and said, "You'd never survive in an elementary classroom. Multiply Shannon's four kids times six and you'll understand why teachers have gray hair before they reach thirty."

"Which brings me to the second reason for thinking of the Florida trip. Between Shannon's kids demanding my time and your teaching demanding your time, we'll never get to be with each other. C'mon, Kelly. Go with me. Just think, four days of lazing around the beach, sipping piña coladas, relaxing."

"Now I know what you do for a living…you work for the Florida Chamber of Commerce," she replied, tempted by his persuasiveness in spite of herself.

He shook his head and laughed at her bad guess. "All weekend I kept thinking, Chad, she's got a problem you can solve. She has a rule book an inch thick and an angel on her shoulder ten feet tall. What the lady needs is for you to take her to a place where there are no rules, where she can be wild as a March hare."

Kelly knew exactly what wild hares did in March. It was their mating season. His presumptuousness knew no boundaries!

Her determination to remain calm, cool and collected was stretched to its limits. She seethed. She counted to ten, then twenty. At thirty-eight she replied sweetly, "Thanks, but no, thanks. I'm busy."

"Doing what?" he asked.

"House-sitting," she improvised. Surely there was someone in her family going somewhere during vacation. Her brothers and sisters always counted on her to be available at a moment's notice. For good measure, she added haughtily, "I have responsibilities...like taking care of Mr. Wiggles. Why don't you find something worthwhile to occupy your mind?"

"Such as?"

"A job. You know, nine to five. Steady employment. I'm certain you've heard of the concept."

Chad laughed as he opened the door for her.

"What's so funny?"

"House-sitting. I get this mental picture of you clinging to a chimney, sitting on the roof of a house."

Kelly wasn't amused . . . much. She bit the inside of her lip to keep from smiling. "In that case, I hope that when you were a teenager you were never hired as a baby-sitter."

He laughed harder and louder.

Teachers standing by their doors like sentries turned and stared at Kelly and the blond, deeply tanned stranger. Their interest was unmistakable.

Kelly concentrated on wiping her feet on the entry mat, hoping to avoid their open stares. She dropped her school shoes from her hand as she put the toe of her left boot on her right heel.

She knew she'd made a terrible mistake when Chad knelt down. Unless she wanted to make a complete ass of herself, she had to let him remove her boots.

Smiling to cover the embarrassment she felt at being the center of attention, she shifted from one foot to the other as needed. When he lightly brushed the palm of his hand across the bottom of her foot to remove any stray pebbles, she felt her toes curl. Then her knees weakened. In imminent danger of losing her balance and completing her humiliation by falling, she put one hand lightly on his shoulder.

She could have walked under the rubber mat when she heard Trudy say, "Congratulations, Kelly. You've finally found a strong man to lean on."

Suppressing a groan, Kelly had the urge to clamp her hand over Trudy's mouth. The sound of Chad's low chuckles and the tingling sensation caused by his hand as it moved from her foot to her ankle to her calf was almost her undoing. His thumb traced the crease at the back of her knee.

Introduce me. Kelly read the unmistakable message in Trudy's eyes. Kelly had taught her first-graders the correct way to introduce a female to a male, but suddenly she couldn't remember whose name came first. Furthermore, the lazy circles his thumb continued to make not only robbed her of her manners but threatened to rob her of her memory. She couldn't think of Trudy's last name.

"H'lo," Chad said, straightening and extending his hand. "I'm Chad Turner, Christy's uncle."

"Oh, yes. I saw you and Christy together Friday afternoon." Trudy fluttered her inch-long eyelashes and put her hand in his. "I commented to Kelly about—"

"Your tan," Kelly quickly said, uncertain that she wanted to have Trudy complete the sentence. When a good-looking man was in the vicinity, her friend had a nasty habit of removing the filter between her brain and mouth, which frequently resulted in total chaos. "Excuse me. I have to clock in."

Kelly grabbed her boots and fled without a backward glance. Let Trudy listen to his charming lies, she thought. From the confidences they'd exchanged, she knew Trudy wouldn't be susceptible to meaningless flattery. Despite the bubblehead role Trudy assumed when she met a "real" man, she always kept her goals in sight.

Trudy wanted a husband; Chad was strictly looking for fun.

Then why had her stomach knotted with tension when she'd noticed how Trudy squeezed his fingers?

Possessive? Me? Ridiculous, she thought. There had to be another rational explanation.

She turned the corner, narrowly missing Phillip and Priscilla.

"Morning," Kelly said, turning sideways to get by them into the office. "I'm early."

She hadn't expected a hearty clap on the shoulders for arriving before the designated time, but a nod or even a grunt would have been greatly appreciated. Funny how Phillip encouraged teachers to praise students and yet seldom gave verbal pats on the back to the teachers.

Kelly selected her card from the vertical tray and inserted it into the time clock. The headmaster and the sixth-grade teacher were so engrossed in their hushed conversation that neither heard the loud clunking sound the machine made.

Hoping the cozy twosome in the doorway would move before she had to brush past them, she fiddled with her time card. From beneath her lowered lashes, Kelly watched them.

No wonder Priscilla gets a superior evaluation, she thought caustically. The woman had goo-goo eyes, breathy laughs and toothy grins honed down to a fine art. Even grading on a performance curve she'd have to give Priscilla an $A+$ for effort above and beyond the call of duty.

From the looks of things, Priscilla had scratched Phillip's name from the potluck list. Frankly, the headmaster wasn't the type of man she thought would attract the flighty teacher, but he certainly seemed to be doing a good job of attracting her this morning.

Automatically Kelly felt sorry for both of them. She'd witnessed her brothers' and sisters' forays into mismatched love affairs. Each time they chose an unsuitable girlfriend or boyfriend, the outcome was the same: heartbreak.

Precisely the reason to keep your distance from Chad Turner, she reminded herself. The chemistry between the two of them was too hot not to cool down.

Students started filing into the corridor, and Kelly cleared her throat noisily. "Here they come."

Straightening his tie, the headmaster stepped into the trickle of incoming youngsters. Priscilla shot Kelly a knowing wink, flipped her hair over her shoulder and sauntered toward the senior wing of the building. Before Kelly headed toward her room, she saw Chad step up to Phillip and introduce himself.

A kindergarten child skipped between the two men, singing, "Tattletale, tattletale hanging by a bull's tail."

Five

———

Time to be a minibanker again, Kelly thought, grimacing. Since this was a short school week that required less lunch money than usual, she couldn't perform the task by rote. With her ears attuned to Jimmy Matthews's account of the snow fort he'd built, and her hands busily stacking quarters into neat piles, her mind should have been too occupied to wander outside the classroom.

It wasn't.

Chad's invitation lured her thoughts away from Jimmy's snowball fight to swaying palm trees and warm sea breezes, to sunshine, sand and a man who could charm and infuriate her simultaneously.

Her hand moved upward from the hard surface of her desk. She fingered the cowl neck of the cherry-red sweater she wore. Although made of synthetic fibers, it had the soothing texture of silk and cashmere. When she'd bought it, she'd known the color was wrong for a near redhead. But once she'd touched the knitted fabric she'd been unable to resist.

Chad Turner's invitation, she told herself, had to be resisted. He probably didn't mean it anyway and never really expected her to accept.

Kelly grinned. She sure wasn't going to rush out after school to shop for an itsy-bitsy bikini. Anyone with half a brain could tell from Chad's voice that the Florida trip was a spur-of-the-moment idea, something to take her mind off the fact that he hadn't bothered to contact her for two days.

Her chin tilted upward defiantly. Even if the invitation had been a serious one, she couldn't have accepted.

Number one, she thought, picking up a pencil and doodling a Roman numeral one on a piece of scratch paper. Beside it she wrote: Florida. Beneath it in outline form she made a capital *A*, then wrote the word Improper.

Trotting off to Florida with Chad would be improper. She hardly knew him, and she wasn't sure that she liked the few things that she did know about him.

The sound of Jimmy's cough as he returned to his seat brought her thoughts back to the classroom. She covered the outline with her hand and rose. "Jimmy? Are you okay?"

"Yes, ma'am. Mom says I don't have a fever."

She quickly scanned his face, looking for telltale signs of the beginning stages of a cold: watery eyes, flushed face, runny nose. Apart from his coughing spell, he appeared healthy.

"Miz Mallory! Me next!" Christy called, waving her hand vigorously.

"Okay, Christy. Tell the class about your weekend," Kelly said, not sure she really wanted to hear it.

She expected Christy to tell about the visitor at her house and knew that if the little girl did so, she'd give a completely unexpurgated version of what was going on. Children had a knack of telling things that would make their parents blush to the roots of their hair if they knew what was being blabbed at school.

There were occasions when she wanted to pry beyond the information a child volunteered. Deep in her heart, Kelly knew this was one of those times. Questions Chad had evaded, Christy would answer with candid innocence. Aware she was actually considering using her position of trust to take advantage of a six-year-old's openness, Kelly felt a wave of guilt washing over her, leaving a tinge of red high on her cheekbones.

She wouldn't resort to underhanded tactics. Down and dirty wasn't her style.

Blond curls bouncing, Christy grinned, scooted from her desk and briskly walked to the front of the room. Bursting with excitement, she wheeled around fast enough to make her ruffled petticoats raise. She giggled, then rocked back and forth from her heels to her toes until her classmates were quiet enough to hear her important announcement.

"Saturday morning my mommy went to the hospital and had a baby brother!"

"Dummy!" a boy called from the back of the room. "Mom's don't have baby brothers."

"Michael, hush!" Kelly reprimanded, but suddenly she realized why Chad had not called her. She felt slightly ashamed of her anger toward him earlier and also embarrassed that she had not even inquired after his sister's health.

Christy put her hands on her hips and stomped one foot. "You're a liar, Michael Simmons! My dad said mommy had a little brother for me to play with."

"Whoa!" Kelly raised her hands to silence both children. She crossed to stand next to Christy. "We don't call each other dummies or liars."

"Everybody knows Michael tells stories. Once he told everybody his dad was Superman in disguise."

"Oh, yeah? I saw you hanging by your knees with your underpants showing!" the little boy yelled.

"Hush! Both of you!" Kelly hadn't raised her voice, but Michael and Christy recognized her stern tone and stopped bickering. "Michael, come here, please."

She dropped to her knees, wrapped her arm around the little girl's waist and extended her other arm toward Michael. She encircled his waist in the same fashion and drew him close. Of the twenty-three children in her classroom, Michael needed to be touched the most. He'd obviously been having problems ever since his parents had filed for divorce nearly a year before. Christy's habitually garbling what she heard was a problem easily corrected. Kelly started with it.

"What's your new brother's name?"

"We picked the name Jason," Christy replied proudly, letting her friends know she'd taken part in naming the baby.

"Do you know when your mom gets to bring him home?"

"Tomorrow," Christy announced, beaming. "Dad says I can hold him if I'm very, very careful. Mom sent a baby doll home from the hospital so I can practice."

She felt Michael lean against her and barely tap her shoulder. "My new mother is going to have a baby," he whispered.

Hugging him closer for reassurance, she whispered loudly, "I have a new baby...well, not a real baby...it's a puppy Todd gave me. His name is Mr. Wiggles."

"What's his first name?" Michael asked.

Kelly put her finger to her cheek and replied, "Do you know what? He doesn't have one. Maybe that's why he doesn't come to me when I call him."

Small hands popped into the air and waved frantically.

"Shelly?"

"Let's have a name-the-dog contest."

"Yeah!" the kids chorused.

"That sounds like fun." She gave Christy and Michael a swift hug and patted their backsides, which meant they should go back to their seats.

"What does he look like?" asked another child. "We can't name a poodle Killer."

"He's hard to describe," Kelly said as she straightened. "I could take a picture and bring it to school."

"Why don't I go to your house and get the pup for you?"

Absorbed in solving Christy's and Michael's dispute, neither Kelly nor the children had noticed the stranger standing in the doorway until he spoke.

"Yeah!" the children chimed enthusiastically.

Although she wasn't opposed to the idea, it irritated her that Chad had been the person to suggest it. She'd have gotten a pet pass from the office before getting her student's hopes up.

Belatedly she wondered what he was doing there and how long he'd been observing. Phillip had a strict policy regarding "intruders" in the building. Children's pets were considered intruders, too.

"Can he go get the puppy?" Alice, a child who rarely spoke, asked.

"First we'll have to get permission from the office. No groans, please," she added when she heard a few disgruntled moans. "Christy, isn't our visitor a special friend of yours?"

Christy's head bobbed up and down. "He's my uncle. Can I introduce him?"

Kelly nodded, giving permission.

Skipping to the door, she tugged Chad's hand until he was front and center in the classroom. "This is my Uncle Chad...Mr. Turner." Giving Michael a meaningful glance, she tacked on, "He's my mother's brother. He calls Mom Princess, and she calls him Prince Charming...that's cuz they're brother and sister. Since he isn't my brother, I call him Uncle Charming. That's right, isn't it, Michael?"

Michael shrugged his thin shoulders. "You should call him Uncle Chad all the time."

Before another skirmish began, Kelly walked to her desk, asking, "Who'd like to take a note to the office? Alice?"

Picking up a pencil and the scratch pad, Kelly felt herself begin to blush. As inconspicuously as possible, she wadded up the top page and shoved it into her pocket. From the grin on Chad's face and the wicked wink he flashed in her direction, she could have sworn he had X-ray vision.

Eagerly approaching the desk, Alice waited until Kelly had finished writing, then said quietly, "He'll say no."

"Who, sweetheart?"

"The headmaster, Mr. Wadsworth. My friend in Mrs. Maxwell's class wanted to bring a puppy to school. He said, 'This isn't a barnyard. No pets allowed.'"

Kelly was afraid Alice was right. She hated to disappoint the children. Unless someone could convince Phillip of the educational value of bringing a pet to

school, the chance of getting permission was somewhere between slim and none.

Who better to ask permission than the person who
came up with the brilliant idea? she mused. Let Chad
be the one to break the bad news to her students.

"Ah, Mr. Turner, would you mind going with Alice
to the office?" Kelly requested sweetly. She checked
her lesson plan book and gave directions to her class.
"While they're gone, we'll start the reading groups.
It's the Tigers' turn on the headsets." Seven children
rushed to the back of the room. "Elephants, today
you start with the game box. Pair off, choose something from the box. Please, keep your voices down to
a dull roar." Another small group dispersed to the
back of the room. "Chipmunks?" The remaining
children ran toward the front of the room. "Keith, you
be group leader."

Kelly walked Alice and Chad to the door. In a soft
voice, she said to Chad, "I hope your charm works."

"I'm here making myself useful, aren't I?" he responded, remembering how easily he'd fast-talked the
headmaster into allowing him a visitor's pass. Flattery hadn't succeeded with Kelly, but it had worked
surprisingly well with her boss. That, and alluding to
the possibility of establishing a fund to buy costly
equipment for children with learning disabilities, had
earned him the freedom to roam throughout the
building.

"Good luck."

Faking supreme confidence, he said, "Why don't you give me the key to your house? I can pick up the pooch and be back within half an hour."

She was tempted to warn Chad to save his breath. He'd be blue in the face before Phillip consented to bend the rules.

"Okay," she agreed affably. She opened the teacher's locker in the corner by the door and fished her keys from her purse. She repeated his favorite parting phrase as she handed him the keys, "See you."

Alice solemnly shook her head. "He isn't gonna let you go get the puppy."

Taking the little girl's hand, Chad started down the corridor. The last thing Kelly heard was Chad telling Alice the story of "The Little Engine That Could."

Kelly returned to the classroom and pulled up a pint-size chair in the reading circle. The wadded piece of paper in her pocket pressed against her upper thigh, and she had a strange urge to revise her Florida list.

Five minutes later, Alice silently slipped into the room and joined her reading group at the headsets behind the lockers. The little girl's expression had been transformed to one of excitement and happiness. She obviously was having trouble sitting still, but Kelly, absorbed in the lesson she was teaching, didn't notice the youngster returning to the classroom.

"What are the two golden keys that will unlock the word?" Kelly asked softly.

"Sound it out."

"What word would make sense there."

"Very good," Kelly said. "Let's use those keys to unlock the word."

While the children used their skills to figure out the new word they'd come across, she glanced toward the door, then at her watch. A worried frown wrinkled her brow. One way or another, Alice should have returned.

"I unlocked it! I know it!" called out two of the six children in the group.

Kelly put her index finger over her lips. "Just a minute. Give the others a chance to use the keys."

Soon all six children had unlocked the word. "What is it?"

"Farm!" they exclaimed in unison.

"Are there any other keys we could have used?"

"The picture."

"What animals do you see?"

"Ducks."

"Cows."

"Chickens."

"Look on page six, Miz Mallory. I found the word duck." Kelly flipped her teacher's manual to the right page. "Good try, Tony. But look at the final sound. What is it?"

"A *g* sound." His small face brightened. "Not duck, dog."

Looking up, Kelly smiled brightly. "Children, we have more company."

All eyes in the room turned toward the door as it closed behind Chad. In an instant, all the children were running toward the door.

"Everybody on the floor in a circle," Chad called. His voice rang with a mixture of authority and panic. He valiantly juggled Mr. Wiggles from one hand to the other while trying to avoid the stampede. "Sit Down!"

Like the professional she was, Kelly took charge of the situation without uttering a threatening word. She moved to the wall and flicked the light switch. Instantly the children dropped to the floor, sitting Indian-style, and put their fingers to their lips, giving the All Quiet signal. The classroom sounded like a giant-size boiler with a pint-size leak. When she flicked the lights again, the shushing sound ceased.

"You do the honors," Chad said, handing her the puppy as though it were a living trophy. "I'll watch."

"Scared?" she mouthed.

He read her lips, grinned and mouthed, "Petrified."

He eased into the straight-backed oak chair behind the teacher's desk. Propping his elbows on her desk, he cupped his face in his hands. Ten minutes of keen observation taught him more about Kelly Mallory than he'd learned about other women he'd dated for months.

Her students gravitated closer and closer to her— just as he had—until they were within touching distance. Maybe it was the soft tones of her voice that made everything she said seem important, he thought. Instead of laying down the rules regarding the care of a small pet, she encouraged the children to relate stories about pets they had at home. Right or wrong, every child was allowed to speak.

Mr. Wiggles was in seventh heaven. Small, gentle hands carefully passed him from one child to the next. Puppy kisses washed hands and faces as his tail wagged nonstop.

Fascinated, Chad watched as two children moved a tripod stand holding a huge tablet and markers to the edge of the circle. One by one, each child wrote a word or short sentence on the page that related to pet care. Not one child hesitated, because Kelly encouraged them to help each other with difficult spellings.

A lanky blond boy took the red marker. Obviously having difficulty, the boy wrote with almost agonizing slowness. The child reminded Chad of himself at that age. Partially buried memories surged into his mind.

Chad vividly recalled a time when he'd stood in front of a green chalkboard feeling totally stupid. He'd been assigned the simple task of copying sentences from the front board to the chalkboard at the side of the room. He'd tried. God, how he'd tried. Squinting his eyes, beads of perspiration on his forehead, he'd really tried to figure out if the first letter was *g*, *b*, *p*, or *d*? To hide his inability, he'd dropped the chalk. It was better for his buddies to think he was clumsy than that he was dumb. Four pieces of broken chalk later, his classmates had been giggling. Inspired to give a better performance, he'd juggled three pieces of chalk and started clowning outrageously.

Cold sweat trickled from Chad's armpit down his side. Blood pounded in his head. A shudder ran down his spine. As though shot from a cannon, he stood. His chair toppled backward, crashing to the floor.

The sound brought him to his senses, putting him back in control.

Righting the chair and grinning like a self-conscious idiot, he apologized for disturbing the class. Politely excusing himself, he skirted around the circle and left the room.

Stunned by Chad's actions, Kelly sat back on her heels, staring at the empty door.

What had happened?

What had she done to cause his phony smile and stuttered apology?

Did he disapprove of the way she was conducting her class?

No, she thought, shaking her head. Disapproval wasn't what she'd seen in his eyes; there had been a look of pain. His entire body had appeared tense. Jerky steps had marked his hasty departure. It was as if something had panicked him.

Michael, patting her knee to get her attention, ended her speculation. She leaned down when he crooked his finger and cupped his hand to the side of his mouth.

"Mr. Wiggles is running around in circles. You know what that means?"

"No," Kelly replied.

Grinning, Michael answered his own question, then made a suggestion.

"You'd better take him outside," Kelly agreed. Glancing at the clock on the back wall, she clapped her hands and said, "It's almost time for art class. Everybody back to their seats, please."

Chad folded his arms over the steering wheel and breathed heavily. "Coward," he muttered. He had acted like a child, like the child he'd been more than twenty years before.

Repressed feelings had returned, and they'd been more powerful than ever. Fear, hurt and anger still washed over him as he swallowed to decrease the size of the lump in his throat.

"I hate school," he heard himself saying years before. "I'm never going back there. Never!"

"You have to go to school."

Chad squeezed his eyes shut to erase the picture of his father standing beside his bed, urging him to get up and get dressed.

"I'm sick."

"Sick of school?" his father had asked.

"Yesssss!" Under the covers he'd dashed the tears from his cheeks with the back of his hand and did his best to stem the flow.

"I promise, son. By fourth grade—"

"Fourth grade?" he'd moaned. "I can't get out of first grade! I'm the biggest kid in the class—and the dumbest!"

"You aren't dumb."

"Then how come I can't do the things other kids do? I can't read. Can't write. I can't even color a stupid picture without going out of the lines."

"I had the same problems at your age." His father had pushed the bedcovers back. "I'm not dumb, am I?"

"No, but I am. I'll never be like you." Chad remembered that at first he'd resisted being folded into his father's arms, but within seconds his nose had been pushed against his father's chest. "I'll never be a lawyer like you."

"If that's what you want to be, you'll be the best attorney west of the Mississippi. I promise."

Sometimes his Dad's promises had convinced him to face another day of ridicule from his classmates. On other days Chad had managed to persuade his parents that he was truly sick. He remembered trying almost anything—headaches, stomach cramps, ragged breathing—whatever it took to avoid going to school.

Now he considered himself one of the lucky ones. He'd outgrown his learning disability.

His father's promise had come true. In fourth grade it was as though a light had come on in his head, illuminating the darkness until his handicap dissipated into nothingness. Skills previously beyond his grasp became child's play.

In one year he'd flown from the "Wrens" reading group up to the "Bluebirds." Excellent grades gave him a new sense of self-worth, and with time he understood what his problem had been.

His tunnel vision, poor small-muscle coordination and inability to transfer written words from one surface to another had been caused by the tissue between his brain and skull not being thick enough. As he had matured and the tissue had thickened, his learning disability had faded into oblivion.

Chad remembered how his father's promise had become his goal in life. He had worked like a demon to earn his father's approval, and had struggled for years to become a lawyer. Eventually he had succeeded. By then everyone had forgotten the trauma of his first few years in school.

Everyone but Chad.

He recalled how, despite self-assurance and charm, he sometimes felt inadequate and afraid. At times all the old feelings of inferiority came tumbling back.

It had not been until after his father's death, that Chad had realized he'd spent most of his life trying to prove to himself that he was an adequate human being, that he was as good and as smart as everyone else.

Speaking of his father, Chad's mother had said, "He wanted you to be taller, better than he was. It bothered him that you chose to follow in his footsteps because he knew it wasn't your own choice. You were doing it to prove something that never had to be proved. Loving completely means you don't have to prove your worth. He wanted you to believe in yourself, to forge ahead of him, to follow your own lead."

Later, after much soul-searching he'd withdrawn from his father's law firm. Since then he'd followed the dictates of his own heart, without making explanations or feeling remorse for the years he'd wasted.

The majority of the people who measured success or failure in dollars and cents would have decreed him worthy, but he no longer cared what they thought. He owned his own business; his bank account was healthy. He'd made it through the tough times and come out on top.

Rubbing his forehead, he whispered, "Loving completely means you don't have to prove your worth."

Had his attack of school phobia after all these years been brought on by his eagerness to prove himself to Kelly? Good Lord, had he reverted to his old pattern of behavior to impress her, to gain her approval? If so, why?

He looked in the rearview mirror and stared at the image there. The reason wasn't shrouded in darkness. It was as plain as the nose on his face. He couldn't deny it, although certainly he *wanted* to deny it. He closed his eyes to avoid it.

Sometimes he had to close his eyes to see the light. He pictured Kelly Mallory. Brilliant blue eyes. Dark auburn hair, with golden highlights haloing her heart-shaped face. Soft clothing, with a hint of sensuality that could drive a man crazy.

"Miz Mallory," he whispered. "Kelly."

The class clown had done the unthinkable—he'd fallen in love with the schoolteacher.

Six

Kelly closed the door in the teacher's lounge and smiled at Trudy, whose class was in the multipurpose room with the physical education teacher. Then she circled the worktable in the middle of the room and sat down. Red pencil in hand, she began grading a batch of papers.

"That smile on your face have anything to do with a handsome guy that I saw going into your room carrying a puppy?" Trudy grinned slyly. "Did you go out with him this weekend?"

"Yes and no," Kelly replied, answering Trudy's questions in order. Over the years she'd become used to her friend asking questions back to back. "How was your date with George?"

"So-so." Trudy plucked the pencil from Kelly's fingers. "No date, huh?"

"No. But during show-and-tell Christy said her mom had a baby Saturday morning. Chad didn't make any explanations as to why I didn't hear from him, but..." She snatched the pencil back and drew a smiling face at the top of the page. "It's pretty clear he was baby-sitting Christy and the other kids while his sister's husband was at the hospital."

"Makes sense. What doesn't make sense is his being in your classroom with a four-legged animal. He must be some sort of miracle worker to get away with breaking two of Phillip's hard-and-fast rules."

Kelly nodded. She had other reasons for believing Chad Turner was a miracle worker. While she'd walked down the hall, she'd given serious thought to vacationing in Florida.

"You just drew a smiling face on a paper that looks like hen scratching. Care to tell me what's going on behind that daydreamy look on your face?"

"Sunshine and ocean breezes." Giving up on grading the papers, she put down the pencil. "Florida."

Trudy looked at her suspiciously. "Okay," she said. "Spill the beans. What's going on?"

Grinning impishly, Kelly lowered her voice to a whisper. "What would you say if I told you Chad Turner invited me to—"

Trudy reached across the table and clamped her hand over Kelly's mouth. Her head jerked toward the heating duct that led from the lounge into the office. "Shh! Phillip!"

Kelly leaned even closer to Trudy and whispered, "Go to Florida with him."

"You can't!"

"I can."

Trudy plopped back in her chair as though she'd been punched in the chest. Eyes bugged out, she shook her finger in Kelly's direction. "You can't. You're the wedding-march, solid-gold-ring, happily-ever-after type of woman."

"I can't believe a toad-kisser said that," Kelly protested, chuckling at the shocked expression on Trudy's face. "Aren't you the one who told me about caviar and champagne?"

"You're mashed potatoes and fried chicken," Trudy proclaimed with a gasp.

"Be honest. Would you tell Chad Turner to kiss off?"

Trudy plowed her fingers through her short hair. "Good grief! I've created a sex-crazed Frankenstein! Forget everything I've said," she pleaded.

"Why?"

"Because he'll break your heart!"

"Biologically impossible," Kelly scoffed, thoroughly enjoying playing the devil's advocate. "Hearts don't break."

Trudy groaned. "I can't believe we're having this conversation."

"Me, either."

"You've just been pulling my leg, haven't you? You aren't seriously considering having a wild fling, are you?"

Picking up her papers and pencil, Kelly glanced at the clock. "Time to get back to the little darlings."

"You aren't leaving this room until you answer my questions." Trudy stationed herself between Kelly and the door.

With an enigmatic shrug of her shoulders, Kelly sidestepped her friend and opened the door. She strolled down the corridor humming "Moon over Miami."

"What'd I do with them?" she muttered as she rummaged through her purse, then her desk, searching for her car keys. She cast a glance at Mr. Wiggles. Happily exhausted, the minute the classroom had emptied he'd curled up in his box and fallen asleep. "You're a big help."

Suddenly she remembered when she'd last had them. She'd given Chad her keys. He'd departed in such a rush he'd forgotten to return them.

"Great! Friday I had keys and no car; today I have a car and no keys."

Left with the choice of walking home or calling Chad at his sister's house, she opened her grade book to the page listing her students' names, addresses and phone numbers. She scribbled the number on her notepad.

For the tenth time she wondered why he'd run out of the room like a scalded dog. His forgetting to return her keys was another indication that the panic she had read in his eyes had been real. Chad's unexpected vulnerability touched that special place in her heart reserved for troubled kids.

She folded the slip of paper, checked on Mr. Wiggles to make certain he was still sleeping, then headed down the hall.

Just as she walked into the office, Phillip hung up the phone. He ripped a page from the pink message pad and handed it to Kelly.

"That was Mr. Turner. He'll be here in a few minutes to return your keys."

"Thanks for allowing Mr. Turner to bring the puppy to school." Phillip's staring at her as though she was something other than a functional piece of school equipment unnerved her. He leaned back in his swivel chair, his fingers steepled over his vest. "Uh, educationally speaking—" she began.

"What are you doing on Thanksgiving?"

"Thanksgiving?" she asked, her voice surprisingly squeaky.

Phillip smiled one of his rare smiles. "Turkey Day?"

Her brain shifted into high gear, but her throat constricted. Did Phillip know about Chad's invitation? Holy moly, he was giving her the same look she'd seen him give Priscilla.

"Uh, yes, Thanksgiving." She swiped her damp palms down the side seam of her wool slacks. A big black lie stuck in her throat. *I'm spending the holidays with my family.* Chad had been introduced as "Uncle Charming," but she couldn't stretch the truth far enough to include him in her family. She swallowed the lie. "I haven't made definite plans."

"Good." The chair's springs creaked as Phillip's weight shifted forward. "Holidays can be especially lonely for unmarried members of the faculty."

Certain he was going to invite her to share Thanksgiving dinner with him, Kelly stepped backward. What about Priscilla? she wanted to shout.

"Priscilla kindly offered to fix turkey dinner for both of us, but she's had to change her plans. Being an only child, she couldn't disappoint her parents when they insisted she spend the holidays in Georgia."

Second choice, Kelly said to herself, none too pleased with his disclosure. First choice would soon be winging her way south, so that left Phillip to find his turkey dinner elsewhere. Tempted to tell him that her table was too small to accommodate more than one stuffed turkey, she kept her cool by saying inanely, "Oh?"

His brow furrowed, which told her that wasn't the response he'd expected. Kelly looked quickly toward the door, hoping Chad would magically appear before Phillip's hints changed into a direct question.

The doorway remained empty. What'd you expect to hear? she asked herself. The sound of bugles, pounding hooves, the arrival of the calvary? No such luck for you, babe.

"I've never stuffed a turkey," Phillip confided. "I'll bet your Thanksgiving turkey looks like a picture in *Gourmet* magazine."

Kelly grinned at his new tactic. "More like the picture on the box of a frozen TV dinner."

"No problem. Anyone who can read can follow a recipe."

Stalemate. She couldn't escape graciously. She also couldn't tell her boss of her tentative decision to fly to Florida with Chad Turner. Taking a leaf from Chad's book, she decided to be evasive.

"In that case, you should be able to fix a superb dinner. There are several single teachers on the faculty. Let's see. There's Trudy, Claire, the new fourth-grade teacher..."

Lips turned downward, Phillip said, "Miss Tucker."

"Yes. Lizzy Tucker." A wicked gleam entered Kelly's eyes. Miss Tucker was the perfect old-maid schoolteacher. "She made those delicious brownies for PTA. Terrific cook. You could ask her to bake the turkey and the others to bring covered dishes. It could be a real potluck dinner!"

"Kelly, that isn't what I had in mind."

"No?" she asked with wide-eyed innocence. "But you said you wanted to share Thanksgiving dinner with other lonely teachers. What exactly did you have in mind?"

His smile said it all.

Last week a shudder wouldn't have run up her spine. She'd have accepted any invitation he issued. *Almost* any invitation, she told herself. Now the thought of an intimate dinner with Phillip sounded stultifying, especially compared to spending a few days with Chad.

Taking a deep breath to fortify her courage, she said, "I appreciate your thoughtfulness, but no, thank you."

"No?" Phillip repeated, apparently shocked by her response. He looked at her questioningly.

Kelly wondered why her answer seemed so hard to understand. Did he think his invitation was irresistible? He got up, towering over her, but she stood her ground. He couldn't intimidate her unless she let him.

He looked as if he was going to approach her, but stopped, stared at her as though he wasn't sure exactly what she was, then returned to his chair.

The first stab of guilt hit her almost instantly. She could relent. It wasn't as though she'd promised Chad she'd go to Florida. In fact, she'd refused Chad's invitation, too. Maybe the reason for his panic in her classroom was that he wanted to retract his invitation before she changed her mind. Perplexed and wondering if she should simply refuse both men and spend Thanksgiving alone, she chewed her bottom lip.

Through lowered lashes she watched Phillip pick up an attendance report.

"Flu bug is going around," he said in his usual clipped voice.

She should have realized that despite Phillip's shortcomings he was a professional, tough but fair. And like most super-organized administrators, he compartmentalized his life: invitation for a turkey dinner in one file folder, attendance records in another.

"Yes, sir."

What passed for a tiny smile flickered on his lips. "Don't forget to clock out, Miss Mallory."

Considering herself dismissed, she said, "Good night."

Smiling, feeling proud of herself, she briskly strode back to her room. Impulsively she stopped just inside the door beside the six-foot-tall alligator she used to measure the growth of her students. She kicked off her shoes and backed up against the wall. Marking her height with her finger, she turned around and looked at the number. Sixty-four inches.

"Self-esteem isn't measured in inches," she said aloud. She felt taller, invincible, ready to conquer the world.

Hearing her voice, Mr. Wiggles sat up, yawned and leaped from the box.

"Yeah, Mr. Wiggles." She scooped the puppy up into her arms. "I could have been a chump and offered to cook dinner for Phillip—for the entire faculty. But I didn't. I didn't volunteer for extra duty, either. Aren't you proud of me?"

Wiggles licked her jaw.

"Wanna steak for dinner? Raw?" she asked, chuckling. She held the puppy in one arm while she put on her boots, gathered her belongings and retraced her steps down the corridor. "No? You want puppy crunchies? Okay, sweetheart, crunchies for you and caviar and champagne for me."

She slipped into her coat when she saw Chad's Mercedes pull into the circular drive. Still feeling euphoric, she rushed through the door. The steps had been cleared, so she hurried toward him.

"Hi! Thanks for remembering you'd taken my keys." She walked around the car in time to see his glum expression change to one of utter delight. Her steps slowed as she savored his smile.

"Hi, yourself. Good day?"

"The best."

"I'm chief cook and bottle washer while Jeff, my sister's husband, visits her and the new baby." He dangled her keys between his fingers. "Why don't we drop your car off at your place?"

Kelly extended her hand, palm-upward. She knew there were clouds overhead, but she could smell sunshine. "And then what?" she prompted.

"My specialty."

One of his hands captured hers as the other placed her keys in the center of her palm. His brown eyes made heavenly promises as he looked at her. Her imagination ran wild. Undoubtedly he specialized in things she'd only read about in books.

"What's that?" she asked, her vocal cords barely responding.

One finger at a time, he curled the keys into her hand. They remained warm from having been in his pocket.

"Chili dogs."

"Chili dogs?" she repeated, letting him pull her hand toward him.

"Wieners. Buns. Chili. And Cokes."

It sounded like caviar and champagne to her ears.

Wiggles, true to his name, wiggled from her crooked arm and leaped toward Chad, who broke the spell when he dropped her hand to catch the flying puppy.

Kelly knew she had a sappy grin on her face, but she couldn't help it. Watching Chad nuzzle the puppy against his smoothly shaven jaw did peculiar things to her pulse.

"No chili dogs for you, buster. We'll let Christy dog-sit."

Chuckling, remembering how he'd teased her about house-sitting, she shook her head. "She'll squash him."

"After your pet-care lesson? No way. Champ will be in good hands." He draped his free arm across her shoulders and whispered, "Let's get out of here before I forget where we are and how cold it is."

An hour later, they'd fed Shannon's four children wieners roasted in the fireplace and dribbled with chili from the slow cooker. The kids were devouring ice cream bars while Kelly sipped a coffee concoction of Chad's. It tasted of cinnamon, sugar, whipped cream and a mysterious ingredient from the liquor cabinet that warmed her down to her toes.

Christy and her younger sister took Wiggles to their room to watch their favorite television program. After a minor scuffle, the boys loaded the dishwasher and adjourned to the playroom to annihilate each other with computer games.

Stretched out next to Chad on the carpet in front of the fireplace, Kelly feasted on more than the food he had provided. He lay on his back, arms crossed behind his head; she lay on her side, curved toward him. His eyes were closed; a satisfied smile was on his face. Strands of blond hair had fallen forward on his wide forehead. She saw one flaw that marred his otherwise perfect features.

"When did you break your nose?"

"Fifth grade."

"Fighting?"

"Fell off my skateboard." His eyes opened lazily. He picked up her hand and placed it on his chest over his heart. "I was showing off for my teacher."

Kelly grinned, loving the way he smiled even while he spoke. "You had a crush on her?"

"Probably." Eyes half-closed, he watched the firelight play in Kelly's hair. Recklessly, without thought of the consequences, he lightly fingered the lock falling over her shoulder. He rubbed her hair between his thumb and forefinger. Warm satin, he mused, threading the shining strands between his fingers. "Your hair matches the fire."

His light caress gave her the excuse she needed to brush his hair back from his brow.

"You're pressing your luck," he warned. His thumb made erotic circles below her ear. "I've wanted to kiss you—really kiss you—since I saw you pulling on Christy's boots."

"Her brother's boots," Kelly corrected automatically.

Her heart seemed to be swelling in her chest, making it difficult to breathe, cutting off the oxygen to her brain. If she'd been thinking straight, she'd have been worried about the children popping into the room. But Kelly wasn't thinking. Period.

Did he raise up? Did she lean down? Or both? Was the spinning, dizzy sensation caused by his turning her onto her back?

Nothing registered other than his mouth sweetly covering hers.

Chad sampled her lips like a connoisseur of fine women. He curbed the driving, primitive male instinct for immediate gratification. Nothing would have pleased him more than to thrust his tongue deep inside her, to learn all her secrets. But he contented himself with pleasing her.

Through his thin cotton shirt he felt her nipples harden as he alternately nibbled her full lower lip, then soothed the love bite with the tip of his tongue. Responding to his leisurely provocation, she parted her lips.

Somewhat shyly, the tip of her tongue followed his. Eyes closed, she touched the planes and hollows of his face. Fine sandpaper skin taut over his square jaw and silky lashes. Her fingers traced the curve of his ear. She thought she'd know him blindfolded.

"Kelly?" he whispered when her light ministrations threatened to spoil his good intentions. Although they were touching from waist to shoulders, he purposely held his lower body away from her. His senses were sending messages too strong to ignore. He wanted her—badly. Or—more precisely—wonderfully.

Her hands burned a fiery path as they moved from his face to his sides, then skimmed over the muscles of his back. "Mmm?"

He rolled onto his back, bringing her with him. Her eyes opened at the sudden shift in position. In a momentary flash, she saw his expression change from one of intense concentration to his usual sunny smile.

"Show-and-tell could be very interesting tomorrow if we're not careful," he warned.

"At open house in September I tell the parents I'll believe half of what I hear in show-and-tell if they agree to believe half of what they hear about what's happened at school."

Brave words, but he noticed she'd straightened until her back touched his thighs. Her hand brushed at her shoulder-length hair to restore order to the places he'd mussed. His eyes strayed to her breasts. Her nipples were clearly discernible. The hand he rested on the curve of her waist slipped beneath the ribbing of her red sweater. Her flesh felt hot beneath his fingers.

Her arms dropped instantly. With one hand she braced herself upright; with the other she covered his wrist, sliding across the golden hairs of his forearm as his palm moved upward under her sweater.

"Stop," he mouthed, unable to speak.

Common sense told her to nod. Unexpectedly she shook her head. She squeezed her eyes shut at the exquisite pleasure she felt when he teased her nipple. Fire seemed to explode behind her eyelids.

"Open your eyes, sweetheart."

"To keep one eye on the door?" she asked in a brief moment of sanity.

"No. I'll hear them on the steps long before they arrive. I want to see what you're feeling."

"Then I want to keep them closed. You're turning me inside out."

"I love your honesty." He heard the small noise in the back of her throat as he began to knead her breasts gently. "You're so damned perfect."

"Is that a complaint?"

"Uh-uh. It wasn't flattery, either. You fit perfectly in the palms of my hands."

His fingers made light work of the front fastening of her bra. Her shoulders shuddered, then sagged forward when he cupped her bare flesh. She gripped his shirtfront tightly with one hand, wadding and un-wadding it weakly echoing the motion of his hands.

Chad moved until he was slouching against the front of the sofa. Her legs bent until her upper thighs fitted snugly against his hip; his forearm touched her waist and the feminine rounding of her stomach. And his elbow wedged intimately between her thighs.

"Now," he whispered, "we're getting closer to ultimate perfection."

Her mouth found his with unerring accuracy as the achy feeling low in her stomach grew. He'd created a hunger within her that couldn't be satisfied by slow, teasing kisses.

Her lips felt cool to Chad, but her breath was hot. Boldly his tongue courted hers. Swirling and darting, advancing and retreating, enticing her to sip and hold on to him. His groan of yearning was answered by a small, hungry sound that seemed to vibrate his very soul.

Maybe the sound was a blessing in disguise.

He'd lost track of who they were, where they were, and the dangerous waters they were swimming toward. He pulled away, but not before he had spread apologetic kisses along her burning cheek.

"I didn't think this could happen to me," he said hoarsely. "I'm acting like a callow kid."

"It isn't supposed to happen like this," Kelly said without thinking.

Chad found the sensitive spot beneath her ear and kissed it. Reluctantly he moved his hand to her hip. "It?"

Realizing she'd spoken her thought aloud, she opened her eyes, then blinked to clear the haze of passion that lingered. "It." *Love, lust—whatever.*

"Interesting pronoun. Sci-fi writers build suspense by referring to the monster as 'it.' Inventors secretively call the project they're working on 'it.'" He chuckled. "Naughty boys brag about 'it.' Did you have a particular 'it' in mind?"

"Be serious," she chided.

"Serious? Didn't you notice when you were kissing me that I don't have a serious bone in my body?"

Disinclined to discuss what she'd meant by *it*, she played along with his easygoing banter. "Only funny bones?"

"Nope." He rolled to his feet and extended his hand toward Kelly. "I'm two-thirds lazybones. Which, in a roundabout way, leads me back to my present role in life—baby-sitter. It's time to get the kids to bed. Want to help tuck them in?"

Seven

Later, alone, Kelly tucked woolen blankets under her chin and stared at the ceiling. No answers there, she thought, turning onto her side. She unknotted her fingers and spread them on her pillow.

Why did she feel like throwing a great-granddaddy of a tantrum? One of those smash-the-dishes, scream-and-shout, break-your-toe-kicking-the-doorjamb tantrums.

She rolled to her stomach and gave her pillow a satisfying punch.

"What's wrong with me?"

Those were the same words she'd said earlier when Chad had kissed her forehead, run down the steps and climbed into his car. She should have been feeling ecstatic. She had what she wanted: a slow-blooming romance.

Then why did she feel like tugging her hair out by the roots?

"Frustrated?" It was the only possible answer, unless she was coming down with a terminal disease that caused the sweet achiness that seemed to have spread permanently throughout her slender body.

Terminal libido, she told herself. Since when had her libido relaxed to the point of becoming obsessed with a good-looking man whose main goal in life was seeking fun. She'd always dated serious, intellectual men. Happy-go-lucky fun-lovers weren't her type.

Kelly whacked the pillow again as she realized she'd never officially dated Chad Turner. She couldn't count Friday as a date. Not when he'd literally picked her up off the pavement and taken her home. He hadn't asked her to go out with him over the weekend; no date then. Today's encounter could hardly qualify as a date, either.

Come to think of it, except for the all-too-brief interlude in front of the fireplace, he'd treated her almost like—a sister?

She kicked back the blanket, suddenly too hot. Earlier she'd turned down the heat to conserve energy. Goose bumps formed on her arms and she began to shiver. She pulled the covers back in place. Chad really had blown her thermostat. She couldn't even decide when she was too hot or too cold.

She knew only one thing for certain: she wanted him.

Go to sleep, she ordered herself, and closed her eyes tightly. Visions of a man with sun-streaked blond hair, a man who smelled of sunshine, floated in front of her. She couldn't force herself to fall asleep any more than she could force thoughts of Chad Turner from her troubled mind.

She burrowed her head under the pillow when she remembered Chad's off-the-cuff invitation to Florida. An afterthought, she groaned, silently cursing.

Should I accept, he'd probably take me to Disney World. Wasn't that the most *fun* place to go in Florida? A mental image of Chad holding her hand, bypassing the romantic rides, taking her from one roller coaster to the next made her want to scream.

Years ago, when she'd gone there with her family, her brothers and sisters had coerced her into using her tickets on a roller coaster ride that had been completely in the dark. It had made her heart race and her stomach do somersaults. In fact, she thought, it had been much like the effect Chad had on her nervous system. If she ever went on the ride with him she would probably end up in the emergency room of the nearest hospital. Croaking from heart failure wasn't her idea of *fun*.

Kelly pulled her head from beneath the pillow. The bedclothes twisted around her lower body as she turned onto her back. Swathed like the Egyptian mummy at the St. Louis Art Museum and feeling totally helpless when it came to deciding what to do about Chard Turner, she directed her attention to unraveling herself from the sheet.

After sitting up and straightening the sheet and blanket, she dropped her head into her hands. Chad Turner had unexpectedly popped into her well-ordered life and turned it topsy-turvy with his sensuous touch, angelic smile and sunshine fragrance. Truly bewitched, bothered and bewildered, she decided to quit fighting and let her life proceed in the direction it had taken.

"Go with the flow," she mumbled, quoting one of the kids, who'd shouted those instructions to a buddy trying to get back to his classroom after the dismissal bell had rung.

The sound of the telephone startled her. She looked at the red numbers on her digital alarm clock; it was long past the hour for sociable phone calls. Only emergency calls were made after ten.

"Hello?"

"Hello, yourself. Did I awaken you from sweet dreams of little kiddies reading perfectly from their first-grade primers?"

"No, Tom. I wasn't asleep yet," she said, recognizing her brother's voice instantly. She didn't ask why he'd called. Tom never needed a reason; he simply did what he felt like doing.

"How's the weather in St. Louis?"

"Freezing." His gloating laughter sounded like fingernails screeching down a chalkboard to Kelly. "I don't want to hear about the weather in Florida unless my airline ticket is in the mail."

"Actually, I'm not in Florida. I have a little business deal that's taken me to North Dakota. That's why I'm calling. I need your help."

Kelly braced herself. The thought of him needing her in North Dakota made her teeth chatter. "No, thank you."

"What do you mean, no, thank you? I haven't asked the favor yet."

"It's the 'yet' I'm worried about. I absolutely refuse to spend Thanksgiving vacation in North Dakota, if that's why you called."

"I'd hate for you to miss a golden opportunity."

Pausing, Kelly wondered what trick Tom had up his sleeve.

"Are you there?" Tom asked after several seconds had passed.

"I'm here—where I'm staying."

"You get out of school Wednesday, right?"

"No. Didn't you see the news on television?"

"I'll bite. No, Kelly, I didn't see the news. What'd I miss?"

"Thanksgiving was called off due to a turkey shortage in Missouri. All the biggest turkeys are stranded in North Dakota."

Tom chuckled. "Same old Kelly—loves to hone her wit on my backside, but always there when she's needed."

"No. Whatever it is you're going to ask—no."

"What would you say if I told you I've met your dream man?"

It was Kelly's turn to smile. She'd already met him, and he wasn't in Dakota. "Oh, yeah?"

"Tall, rugged, cowboy. Cattle rancher. A lonely widower."

"With ten kids, right?" Tom's strange notion that she considered her first-graders as substitute offspring was maddening.

"Nope. Two."

"Tom, I appreciate your thinking of me, but sorry, not interested."

"Okay. How about a short, balding, middle-aged department store owner? No kids."

"Brother dear, when are you going to learn that I'm capable of selecting my own man. I don't need big brother to screen my prospective beaus."

Her eyes narrowed as she realized there was more truth in that statement than she'd previously acknowledged. Tom had screened her boyfriends. Each time she'd introduced a male friend to her family, it had been Tom who'd vetoed her choice.

She'd never been seriously involved with any of them but there had been one or two whose company she'd really enjoyed.

"I only want a man who'll treat you right," Tom said, sounding aggrieved at her lack of willingness to meet a man he'd chosen. "After all, I wouldn't want to see you getting set in your ways. School-marmish."

Kelly's self-esteem began to shrivel. Did he think she was a charity case who needed help finding a man? "Don't worry about that."

"Don't get defensive."

"Who's defensive?" she added pointedly. "I can find a nice man without your help."

"That's good to hear."

Kelly smiled. "In fact, Tom, my luck has changed. I've met someone I like very much. He's enough like you to be your blond-headed twin brother."

Kelly heard him gasp, and her smile broadened.

"Yes, indeed, big brother. In fact, the reason I can't do you a favor during Thanksgiving vacation is I'm planning on spending it with him. In Florida, I might add."

"Now hold on. You shouldn't go anywhere until one of us meets this . . . this . . ."

"Yes?" she asked sweetly.

"Dammit, Kelly. I'm flattered that my little sister is dating a man who reminds her of me, but I think you should be careful. Don't rush into anything."

"Don't worry about me, Tom. I'll be fine."

"I could forbid you to go," he said, indicating he was indeed worrying about her.

His threat lacked conviction, and Kelly simply laughed.

"I must say I'm shocked at the willful streak you've acquired," he grumbled. "What happened to docile, keep-the-peace-at-all-costs Kelly Mallory?"

Prickles of guilt traveled up her spine. In one day, she'd shocked two people. Three, if she counted turning down Phillip's dinner invitation. Her laughter wilted. Four, she recalculated. She had to count herself. A few days ago she would never have believed any of this could have happened.

"Eventually everyone grows away from the influence of their family. It just takes some people longer than others."

"Does that mean you aren't going to fetch and carry the load for your brothers and sisters?"

Kelly paused; her mouth worked, but she said nothing. Is that how her siblings saw her? Like a little dog fetching and carrying to get a pat on the head? Her face turned livid.

"I . . . I . . ." she began, searching for a suitable reply.

"You know, Kelly, I take it back. You should do whatever you think is right. That willful streak I mentioned? I do believe it strongly resembles a genuine backbone. You know, I bet you can find Mr. Right without any help from anyone."

The admiration she heard in his voice astonished her. "You aren't mad because I didn't give in and change my plans?"

"Mad?" he hooted. "Hell, no. It was no big deal. I just thought a trip out West would put some giggles into your life."

"Fun," Kelly muttered, wondering if the whole world saw her as a dull chump.

"Whose call-waiting is clicking? Yours or mine?" Tom suddenly asked.

"Mine."

"Hey, I love you."

"Love you, too."

Kelly disconnected his call by pressing the button down. She glanced at the clock.

Two phone calls this late at night? Her luck must be improving. "Hello."

"Hi. This is Chad. I hope you weren't sleeping." Alone in the spare bedroom at Shannon's house, he'd been lying in bed with the taste of her clinging to his lips. He'd known he'd never be able to close his eyes until he spoke with Kelly one more time. He hoped she was having similar difficulties.

Kelly glanced toward the open bedroom door. His voice sounded close, as though he was on the extension in the living room. Remembering her conversation with Tom, she wondered if Chad's ears were burning. "No. The black sheep of the family just called."

"The one I remind you of?"

"Yes. Tom."

"Is that good or bad?"

"Good, for a change. He's in North Dakota. He wanted me to cook Thanksgiving dinner for him."

"That's good?"

Disappointment ripped through him. Tomorrow his sister would return, ending his temporary baby-sitting job. He had one or two business matters to complete; then he'd looked forward to expending his energies on Kelly.

Kelly grinned at the question in his voice. Obviously he didn't think much of Tom's invitation. Curling on her side with the phone cradled between her face and shoulder, she replied, "I declined."

"That's what I wanted to hear," Chad exclaimed enthusiastically.

"Oh?" Kelly said, her heart beating faster. This was the perfect opportunity for him to reissue the invitation to Florida. She prayed he would, hoping he had meant it when he'd told her he wouldn't take no for an answer.

"My sister suggested I invite you for dinner here."

Her hand raised to her throat. He wasn't going to ask her again. She had been a fool to reject his invitation so callously.

"But I'm partial to eating turkey leftovers when the sandwiches come from a picnic basket taken to the beach."

Specks of black swam before her eyes. She couldn't wait for him to ask. "Yes! I'm going to Florida!"

"With me?"

Chad sounded delighted. The two words he uttered somehow made her giddy. "Of course," she said, feeling ecstatic.

"Terrific!" Chad wasn't going to give her a chance to back out. He decided to finalize the deal as quickly as possible, then move ahead before second thoughts could cause complications. "I'll make the arrangements to leave Wednesday evening. Don't worry about the details." He paused briefly to change directions. "I need some professional advice. Christy begged to stay home from school tomorrow because Jason is coming home. School is important, but..."

"Shannon would probably appreciate getting settled in at home without the four kids there. If Christy stays home, they'll all want to skip school. Did she forget that we're starting the contest tomorrow?"

Kelly asked, hoping to supply Christy with a reason to want to go to school.

"No. She has a list of first names for Mr. Wiggles. Jiggles was her favorite. She beaned me with a pillow when I suggested 'Pooch.'"

"Good for her. I can't see myself standing on the front porch yelling, 'Here, Pooch, Pooch, Pooch.'"

"I have to admit that sounds like something a model would say while pinching her waistline testing for flab."

Chad relaxed against the pillow he'd propped against the headboard of the bed and listened to Kelly's soft laughter. If he could bottle the heady feeling it gave him, he'd make his second fortune. And he knew exactly how he'd market it. Eyes closed, he imagined Kelly with her auburn hair spread on an ivory satin sheet. Dressed in a lacy mocha-chocolate gown, she'd raise her arms to beckon a man off-camera. Her enticing laughter and the name of the product would be the only sound. Simple and seductive, he mused.

Blinking, he erased the image. He'd never let anyone see that commercial. He'd never share her beauty with the world. He would retain exclusive rights to that fantasy for all time.

"Are you wearing the high-necked flannel nightgown with the tiny yellow rosebuds?" he inquired huskily.

"No. Mr. Wiggles confiscated it for a makeshift pillow in his bed." Kelly's sense of responsibility surfaced. "Oh, no. I just thought of something. Puppies can't take care of themselves. What am I going to do with him while I'm gone?''

Visions of sleeping with his head resting on Kelly's nightgown shattered. "I'll take care of everything." *Wiggles, Tom, the entire school faculty, if that's what's necessary,* he silently added. Taking Kelly to Florida with him had become his top priority.

Kelly was accustomed to taking care of details. Her family, friends and acquaintances had always been happy to let her tidy up loose ends. Chad's voluntarily lifting the smallest burden from her shoulders was a new experience.

Uncle Charming, she thought, and smiled. Feeling delectably cherished, she snuggled under the covers. She'd have to be careful, or letting him take care of her could become habit-forming.

She covered her mouth to smother a yawn.

"Are you going to appear out of nowhere tomorrow?" she asked wistfully. She thought she heard him murmur, "I'll be wherever you need me," but she wasn't certain. He'd yawned, too.

"G'night, sweetheart," he said.

Kelly smiled. "'Night."

Replacing the receiver in the cradle, she wrapped her arms around the spare pillow. She wouldn't remember her dreams; she wasn't that lucky.

Eight

We're going shopping," Trudy declared. To emphasize her point, she snatched Kelly's homework papers from her hand and stuck them in her mailbox. "No argument."

Kelly retrieved them, and a note fell from the box. "I'd planned on a shopping expedition, but I'm not getting behind with my paperwork."

"I'll grade and record them for you," Trudy said, stooping to pick up the pink slip of paper. Without the slightest qualm, she read the telephone message and the bold cursive writing Phillip had added with a red Magic Marker. She grumbled, "The man missed his calling. He should have been a time-and-motion expert," and passed the note to Kelly with her thumbnail piercing the corner where he'd placed a number. "He's actually keeping track of how many personal calls we receive."

Knowing Phillip had read the message Chad had left for her bothered Kelly more than his keeping records on incoming personal calls. His professionalism could be stretched thin over his male ego during their next encounter, she thought.

The message was short and sweet. "Florida trip confirmed. Please call me."

Thanks to the bombshell Christy dropped during show-and-tell, the entire class knew Wiggles was staying with Christy while their teacher gallivanted off to Florida. Fortunately, the class didn't make a connection between Chad's suntan and Florida's sunshine. Phillip wasn't that naive.

Kelly folded the note and stuck it in her purse.

"What's wrong?" Trudy inquired, seeing Kelly frown.

"Muzzles should be legalized. Now I understand why I was getting so many inquisitive stares during lunch today. I must have missed the loudspeaker announcements this morning. The entire building—faculty, administration, students and the custodial staff—must've heard about my trip."

"So?"

"Well, first-graders may have trouble adding one and one, but the adults don't. Did you read the small print in your teacher's contract? What about 'moral discretion'?"

Trudy made a dismissive gesture. "That's like the insubordination clause. If you smack Phillip across the chops during a school assembly, you're insubordinate. Give him a karate chop in the privacy of his office and it's your story against his. Unless you plan on making X-rated films and showing them in the sixth-graders' sex-education class, you don't have a contractual problem."

Blushing, Kelly fumbled with the keys she'd pulled from her purse.

Trudy stooped down for the second time and teased, "Should I just stay down here, or are you finished littering the floor?"

"How'd you like a personalized muzzle for Christmas? I'm ordering them by the gross."

"Make mine hot pink, would you?" Straightening and giving Kelly a saucy smile and her keys, she added, "Speaking of hot pink, I saw the cutest swimsuit at Saks. Let's go there first."

"First I go to Todd's house."

Groaning, Trudy slapped her forehead with the palm of her hand. "I swear, Kelly, I'll have a receding hairline before I'm thirty, and it'll be your fault. Call and cancel your tutoring for today."

"Todd needs extra help. I can't—"

"Skip the dedication lecture. I've heard it so often I know it by heart." Exasperated, Trudy asked, "The malls close at nine. When are we going shopping?"

"Seven?"

"Seven! That only gives us two hours!"

Kelly grinned. "That's about an hour and forty-five minutes over my budget."

"Splurge!"

"I can tell you're an only child. With Christmas just around the corner and scads of presents to buy, I'll be draining my savings account next month.

"Santa will be exhausted from carrying gifts to your door," Trudy replied, a bit envious.

"Nope. Excluding Tom, they're all struggling like me to make ends meet. I told them not to spend their money on me."

Trudy didn't call her a chump, but it didn't take a psychic to read her mind. Taking Kelly by the arm, Trudy marched toward the front exit. "I know you're saving what you don't spend on others for a rainy day. Well, guess what? The weatherman says there's a warm front coming through St. Louis that's bringing in torrential rains. This is it; you're gonna spend a few bucks on yourself for a change."

Kelly opened her mouth to argue, then wisely shut it. She'd treat Trudy exactly as she treated her brothers and sisters when they were being dictatorial: she'd shut up, nod occasionally and do what she wanted to do.

She not only had to tutor Todd, she had to stop by her house to feed Wiggles and take him outside. She'd grab a bite to eat while she graded papers.

They crossed the parking lot with Trudy issuing a time schedule in a voice a drill sergeant would have been proud of.

"...and you'll meet me at the side entrance of Sak's at five-thirty. No later."

Kelly smiled noncommittally. As they both started their engines, Kelly tooted her horn, raised seven fingers and drove toward the exit. Realizing what Kelly meant, Trudy honked her horn and waved five fingers frantically, but Kelly simply shook her head.

When she arrived at Todd's house and parked the car, she realized the old I'm-guiltier-than-sin-for-doing-what-I-want-to-do feeling hadn't hounded her during the drive. She hadn't caved in to Trudy's demands. She'd blithely signaled her intent through the back window without a pang of guilt.

No wonder Trudy had flooded her engine, Kelly thought. Walking tall, she hurried to the front door.

Chad dialed Kelly's phone number for the tenth time. He counted the rings until he reached eight, then hung up. Where is she? School is over at 3:30. She lives less than ten minutes from work. Why isn't she home?

He'd left a message at school. Didn't she realize how impatient he was to hear from her?

Pacing from one end of the kitchen to the other, he looked toward the front door when he heard the doorbell ring. His heart leaped. Bless her heart, she'd come over instead of calling.

Grinning broadly, he strode to the door and flung it open. His grin vanished as quickly as it had appeared.

"Hi, Uncle Chad. Somebody locked me out. Is Mom home?" the little girl asked eagerly. Christy flung her backpack on the small table in the foyer and raced upstairs before Chad could recover.

Christy's defection in favor of her mother was to be expected, but Chad missed hearing her laugh when he swooped her into his arms and gave her a bear hug.

"She's upstairs with company," he said to an empty hallway as he closed the door.

From the time Shannon had arrived carrying her precious bundle, he'd been treated almost like the family butler. His sister's visitors bestowed polite smiles on him when he answered the doorbell, then hurried upstairs to see Shannon. A short while later they had sappy grins on their faces when he escorted them out the door. Each woman walked out looking as though she was the one who'd recently given birth. One elderly lady had the audacity to pinch his cheek and tell him the baby resembled him.

During his next trip into Shannon's room, he carefully examined the newborn. He couldn't find any resemblance. The baby's head was slightly pointed. Tufts of blond hair fringed his ears. Jason opened one eye and screamed until his face was beet red. No, he didn't understand why everybody was making such a big to-do over the tiny baby, nor did he consider the older woman's comment to be a compliment.

At least Christy knows her way up there, Chad thought, rubbing his upper thighs. He must have climbed those stairs forty times. At one point, when several women had arrived one after the other, he'd considered painting yellow footprints on the carpet to direct traffic.

Chad peeked through the sheer curtain beside the door to make certain he wouldn't be interrupted the moment he dialed Kelly's number. Seeing no one, he headed into the kitchen.

"Be there," he whispered, jabbing the correct buttons. On the ninth ring, he gave up.

He heard Christy's feet dragging as she came down the hall. He empathized. "You're going to trip on your lower lip," he teased, pulling her against his legs.

"The lady with Mom shooed me from the bedroom because I have germs." She turned her hands palm upward, then flipped them over. "They must be eeny-teeny."

Pretending to be serious, Chad inspected them. "Let me zee zeem with my X-ray vision." He turned an imaginary knob on the side of his head. "Hmm."

"Lots?" Christy grimaced.

"Hmm. Zgadz."

"Vot are vee going to do?" Christy asked, trying to adopt the same mad-doctor accent.

"Vee vill vait until zee visitor departz. I think zee germs vill go away. Poof!"

"Will they?" Christy asked, truly concerned.

Chad scooped Christy into his arms. "We'll wash your hands to make certain they're gone. Okay?"

"You're the best uncle in the whole wide world." Her small arms gave him a mighty hug. "I love you to pieces."

With considerable fanfare and hoopla, Chad made washing her hands fun. With the new baby grasping everyone's attention in his tiny fist, the four other kids would need an extra scoop of tender loving care.

"How would you like to make an ice-cream sundae?" he asked, crossing to the freezer.

"Before dinner?"

"Does your stomach have a clock inside that jingles when it's ice-cream time?"

"No."

"Would your parents object to your having frozen milk with eggs and sugar?"

Christy grinned, skipped to the table and pulled a chair to the counter. "Uh-uh. There's a chocolate cake one of the ladies brought. I'll bet it has good stuff in it, too, huh?"

"Flour, eggs, milk." *Chocolate, more sugar.* Shannon would scrub the kitchen floor with his face if she could hear him. "You cut the cake; I'll serve the ice cream. Cut pieces for your brothers and sister, too. They'll be home soon."

He glanced toward the phone and shook his head. He'd have to cancel the reservations he'd made at Tony's. No intimate dinner with Kelly tonight. He'd be busy caring for his nieces and nephews until their bedtime.

Dangling what looked to Kelly like two silver Band-Aids attached to twin silver threads in front of Trudy's nose, she asked, "Do women wear these in public?"

"That's not your size; it's too big."

Kelly examined the tag. "This is a twelve? Find one of these in a size eight, would you?"

"It's not your color, either."

"Who said anything about buying it? Whoever designed this read 'The Emperor's New Clothes' one too many times. There's nothing here!"

"G-strings. They're popular with the high school and college kids. Keep looking. We don't have time to play around." Plastic hangers clicked together as Trudy looked for another bathing suit. "Ah-ha! *This* is fantastic! Fishnet is really in style this year."

"Fishnet? A whale could swim through those holes. Now who's playing around?"

"Try it on."

Kelly selected a paradise-print maillot with shirring detail at the hip. "This is cute."

"Cute? I've seen newsreels of turn-of-the-century women on Atlantic City's boardwalk wearing sexier swimsuits. I'd think that coming from such a large family you wouldn't be so modest."

Groaning, Kelly sauntered toward the dressing room. She'd been raised to respect her brothers' and sisters' privacy—that included everything from staying out of each other's diaries to being fully clothed whenever in the presence of another family member. There had been no running around half-naked in her home. In college, where two-thirds of the girls cruised around the dormitory in bras and panties, she'd felt unsophisticated. She'd found a happy medium by wearing ultrafeminine robes. Sleek satin and lace had adequately covered her. By her senior year, many of her friends had been wearing stylish robes, also.

"You're always saying I'm too modest. Next you'll be accusing me of turning out the bathroom lights when I take a shower," Kelly quipped.

Trudy snapped her fingers as though she'd just solved a puzzle. "You must. When we compare electricity bills, yours is always lower. Finally, you've let your secret slip."

"Very funny, Trudy. You keep looking. I'll call when I'm ready to model."

Firmly closing the dressing room doors behind her, Kelly stripped off her outerwear. One glance in the full-length mirror had her wishing her white skin had retained some of last summer's tan. Careful not to let her fingernails puncture the fabric, she pulled on the suit she'd picked. Except for the high-cut legs that exposed her hips and the curve of her buttocks, it flattered her figure. Opening the louvered door, she crossed to the three-way mirror and called, "Trudy, c'mere and tell me what you think."

"Not bad," Trudy commented, circling Kelly. "Those bulky clothes you wear don't do justice to your figure. French-cut legs must have been designed just for you."

"Thanks...I think." Trudy's compliments often bordered on being insults. No malice intended, Kelly reminded herself.

"You didn't like the fishnet suit?"

"Did you read the price tag?"

With a long-suffering sigh, Trudy read the tag. Her eyes widened. "That's two weeks' salary!"

Kelly grinned. "You're stealing my lines. I expected you, the charge-card queen, to rip the tag off and tell me it's un-American to pay cash. You're the only person I know who pays for Christmas in August."

Twisting the hanger back and forth, Trudy said, "We're talking about going over my charge-card limit to pay for this little piece of frippery! I'm surprised the store doesn't charge by the minute just to try this on."

Kelly patted her tummy and took one last look in the triple mirror. She decided the swimsuit she'd chosen fit both her pocketbook and her curves. Over her shoulder she saw Trudy's thoughtful expression.

"Do you still think I shouldn't go?"

Shaking her head, Trudy answered, "Stay here and a certain kindergarten teacher you consider your best friend won't be sharing lesson plans with you."

Their eyes met in the mirror's reflection. Kelly asked, "Why the change of heart?"

"I plead the Fifth Amendment," Trudy mumbled, eyes dropping.

"How could you incriminate yourself?"

"We've been friends since the first day we started teaching." Self-consciously Trudy ran her hands through her hair. "Friends shouldn't feel jealous or envious of each other."

Her jaw dropping, Kelly turned and stared at her friend. "You've got to be kidding. Aren't you the lady who's had more dates this month than I've had in the years we've known each other?"

"Precisely. You'd think the odds of going on a Florida holiday with a dreamboat guy would be in my favor. You're going to think I'm playing with half a deck when you hear who's sharing Thanksgiving dinner with me."

Kelly made an educated guess. "Phillip?"

"Dammit! Who told?"

"Nobody."

"Come on, fess up. After what I said about you dating Phillip, you should have guessed either Richard or George . . . or Rumplestiltskin before you came up with his name. Teachers' grapevine?"

Kelly walked past Trudy toward the dressing room. She pointed to her temple with her forefinger. "A smart teacher knows everything—a veritable walking encyclopedia."

"So what do you think?"

"I've told you what I think of Phillip."

Kelly paused beside a circular rack of cover-ups. She found one with a vivid turquoise color that matched the background of the suit she'd chosen. Pulling up the sleeve, she read the price tag. She could buy a couple of dresses for her nieces for that amount. Her sister, Kathryn—the youngest of the Mallory girls— had recently had a baby boy. She'd feel terribly guilty if she spent the money she'd saved to buy something special for the baby's first Christmas. Kelly gave a wistful sigh as she dropped the price tag.

Trudy followed. She would have squeezed into the dressing room, but Kelly closed the door. Respecting

Kelly's modesty, Trudy leaned against the partition wall.

"Tell me again. Maybe you'll convince me this time."

"He's a nice man. Attractive. Good head on his shoulders. Good job. Fair." She opened the door a crack and looked through it. "I haven't changed my opinion of him. Have you thought of the possibility that Phillip might be completely different socially than he is professionally?"

"That's unlikely. I'm certain the man wears boxer shorts under his three-piece pin-striped suits." Trudy's conjecture brought a chuckle from the cubicle. "Professionally, we do have a lot in common," Trudy said, as if trying to convince herself. "Oh, what the heck, if he gets too stuffy I'll soak him in liquor, pop him in the oven until he thaws and then bring him to the boiling point."

Kelly chuckled. She tried to picture Phillip soused, hot and bothered. She failed. Her vivid imagination wasn't stymied, however, when she thought of what Chad wore beneath his well-tailored slacks. A vision of bikini shorts turned her cheeks rosy red.

"Speaking of . . . unmentionables," Trudy said. "I know I shouldn't ask, but have you thought about sleeping arrangements on your trip?"

"Chad's taking care of the details," Kelly said after a moment's hesitation. She felt herself blushing at her friend's direct question.

"Sounds interesting. What does that mean?"

Trying to laugh, Kelly replied, "I don't know. Maybe he's going to soak me in liquor, pop me in the oven and..."

"You're comparing yourself with Phillip? Forget it. You aren't stuffy all the time like he is."

"Gosh, was that what's known as a backhanded compliment?" Kelly asked drily, very drily. "One more of those and we won't be on speaking terms."

"It came out wrong. Stuffy isn't an ugly word; it just sounded..."

"Please. Don't explain." Dressed in her street clothes now, Kelly breezed out of the dressing room. She kept walking until she reached the sales counter. With a million last minute details to take care of before the trip, she didn't need one of Trudy's heart-to-heart, "I'm-telling-you-this-for-your-own-good" talks.

"But I'm worried about you," Trudy protested, tagging along. Frustrated to the nth degree because Kelly wasn't going to listen to her, much less heed the sage advice she planned on giving, Trudy babbled, "Your trotting off to Florida isn't like going to the corner grocery store. Darn it, Kelly, the whole world may see you as perfect, up for nomination for sainthood, but I know you're vulnerable. Don't you know I *care* about what happens to you?"

Distracted by a saleswoman who greeted both of them, took the swimsuit and the cash, Kelly only heard the words Trudy emphasized when her voice raised: *perfect and sainthood.*

Raging inwardly, Kelly gave Trudy a piercing glare. "You make me sound as though I have some sort of Mother Teresa complex. I don't."

"Prove it," Trudy dared.

"How?"

"By answering one question."

Kelly nodded curtly. "Shoot."

"Are you going to sleep with Chad?"

Nine

I'll do exactly as I please,'' she replied pointedly, practically running through the exit and toward her car in her haste to avoid any more questions from Trudy.

She'd driven out of the mall's parking lot before she realized tears had gathered in the corners of her eyes. Fighting invariably left her feeling shaken and confused.

She should have known better than to let her temper get the upper hand. Despite her seemingly callous questions and comments, Trudy meant well. For the sake of friendship, she should have let Trudy make her point and then gone on about her business without getting upset. She should have been able to take constructive criticism without feeling hurt, Kelly told herself. Her thoughts ground to a screeching halt as she recalled the order of events. Had she decided before consulting Tom and Trudy? Inwardly groaning, she realized she'd told Chad no until after she'd spoken to Trudy and Tom.

Had she subconsciously wanted their approval before accepting? She'd thought she was going to please herself, but...

"No! No! No!" she grumbled loudly. "I wanted to go. I would have gone with or without their blessings! I'm pleasing myself, not them."

Shouting it didn't make it true, she told herself.

Deep down, she realized she might simply be using Chad. To go with him on the pretext of building a relationship when there was the distinct possibility that she was only seeking a pat on the head from someone else was wrong. Between now and Friday, she'd have to sort through her mixed emotions and decide what to do.

She pulled into her drive and cut the engine. Wrapping her arms around herself, she rested her forehead on the cold steering wheel. The tears she'd held in check dribbled down her cheeks. Her thoughts had come back to her parting shot at Trudy. "I'll do exactly as I please," she'd said. Now she wasn't at all sure if she even knew what she pleased to do.

But Trudy's allegations hurt.

Self-doubt assaulted her.

Trudy had said that Kelly acted like some kind of saint. Did the other teachers feel the same way? She'd thought the faculty was close-knit, like a large family.

At home, her brothers and sisters had always been happy to give her a pat on the head for doing unpleasant duties. Didn't the teachers feel the same way? Trudy had indicated they resented her.

She hated the idea of her colleagues thinking she was acting superior when she was only doing her best to get along with everyone. She thought of herself as hardworking; they saw her as a perfectionist. She wasn't interested in angel wings! She simply wanted to be loved.

Feeling totally alone, she navigated her way toward home.

First Tom and now Trudy, she thought, rubbing a tear off as another clung to her eyelashes. Both of them had chided her. And yet, when she'd told them of her plans, both Trudy and Tom had initially opposed the trip. Why hadn't they been ecstatic?

An unwelcome thought entered her mind. Was she going with Chad only because that was what she thought people wanted her to do.

No, she silently told herself, shrinking from the idea. She'd made up her mind before she'd talked to either of them.

Minutes later, when the car was cold and Kelly had begun to shiver she moved. Fumbling in the dark, she pulled a tissue from her purse. Blow your nose and quit blubbering, she told herself. Head lowered, she picked up her package and reached for the door handle.

The door opened before she touched it.

Surprised, she gasped and looked upward. The fragrance of sunshine told her who had opened the door before she saw the hand reaching toward her.

"Where've you been? I've been trying to reach you since—" The soft glow from the gaslight in the front yard lit her face. Although she'd wiped her cheeks, unshed tears glistened in the darkness. His heart twisted as he pulled her into his arms. "Kelly? You've been crying. What's wrong?"

"Nothing." *Everything.* It felt so good to be held by him, she thought, resisting the urge to weep on his chest.

"Whatever it is, we'll talk inside. Give me your keys."

She handed them over without protest. His lips brushed against the softness of her hair as one arm dropped around her shoulders. He gently squeezed her hand. Somehow his very reassurance brought a fresh flood of tears to her eyes. Blinking wouldn't stem the flow.

Chad opened the door, switched on the lights and watched as Mr. Wiggles scampered into the foyer. His arm slipped to his side when Kelly knelt down to pick up the pup.

"Watch it. He'll shred your nylons," Chad warned.

"Unconditional love is worth more than the price of a pair of nylons." Kelly let the puppy kiss away her tears. Between Chad's hugs and Wiggles's kisses, she felt better. "Regardless of how late I arrive or what mood I'm in when I get here, Wiggles is thrilled to see me. Aren'tcha, pup? You love me despite my flaws."

Chad smiled wistfully. Wiggles was a mongrel, a pup with no papers, no pedigree, the runt of the litter. And yet, in the short time Kelly had had the little dog, she had learned to love him. She didn't expect the puppy to be useful. She kept him because she cared about him and because he loved her.

Wouldn't it be wonderful for a man and woman to give and accept love on those terms? he thought.

Could Kelly ever love him that way, he wondered. There was only one way to be sure, and that was to continue letting her believe he was just a charming ne'er-do-well. If she could love him under those circumstances, he'd know that she cared about him and not the wealthy man he'd become. His vow never to prove himself to another person remained intact.

"That's the kind of love we all want," Chad commented sincerely.

The husky timbre of Chad's voice, and his lopsided smile, had a powerful effect on Kelly. Adrenaline surged and her heart seemed to beat too fast.

"I'm not certain unconditional love is possible between people," she replied. "Even when we do our best to earn love, we can fail miserably."

Aware of the pain she felt, he asked, "Is that why you've been crying?"

Returning Wiggles to the floor, she nodded, leading Chad into the living room. Wiggles followed close behind. She motioned for Chad to have a seat on the sofa. When he patted the cushion beside him, she sighed and sat next to him. Wiggles yawned, then lay down on the floor between their legs.

How natural it seemed to feel his arm around her and to unburden herself of her problems, Kelly thought before saying, "I've just about decided it's impossible to earn love. I've done everything I could think of to please my family and friends, but I don't think it's worked."

"Isn't there a line in a song that goes something like...you can't please everybody, so you might as well please yourself?"

The lamp on the end table cast sufficient light to make the red highlights of her hair dance, and his fingers delved into her silky tresses.

"You just cut through the flab right to the heart of the problem." Relaxing, she closed her eyes and let his touch soothe her. "I've been pleasing others for so long that I can't distinguish between what I'm doing to please someone else and what I'm doing to please me."

"Maybe I can help you," he said after a long silence. Slowly, haltingly, he told her about his learning disability. He hadn't been able to tell her the details before for some reason and found it difficult to talk about it now. He felt diminished by it, as if Kelly, as a teacher, would withdraw from him or pity him because of it. But he realized that knowing would help her. "Like most small kids, I wanted to please my parents, and sometimes I was so frustrated I'd pull some pretty outrageous stunts. I was the only kid in the first grade suspended for ten days."

Curious, she asked, "What did you do?"

"Told the kids I had rabies and chased them around the playground snapping my teeth. I bit one kid who sniggered each time I was called on in class." Not willing to minimize the seriousness of his offense, he added, "I drew blood."

Her heart went out to the small boy who'd physically punished another child for mental abuse. She felt certain the bite had healed long before the blows that had landed on Chad's self-esteem.

"Anyway," Chad continued, "I covered up my learning limitations by being the class clown. I couldn't read aloud to save my life, but I could entertain the kids with animal impressions...sometimes impressions of the teacher. Nobody was spared the class clown's pranks...other than my parents. I hated school; the school hated me. Just walking into your building makes me nervous."

"Is that why you ran out of my room while the kids were working on the experience chart?"

Chad nodded. His lips pressed lightly against the crown of her head. He had to remind himself that he was trying to comfort Kelly by telling her of his experience. Having her in his arms severely tested his self-restraint.

"When I saw that tall blond kid having a little trouble it brought back my own experience so vividly I felt like I was seven years old again. I just had to leave. Being the class dummy was traumatic, but worrying about losing my parents' love was the worst part of the problem. I thought my dad set the moon, hung the stars and made the sun rise each morning. I also thought he must have hated me each time the school called.''

"Did he?''

"We're all human, Kelly. His patience and understanding were worn pretty thin when he received at least one call from the principal each week. Dad was a trial attorney,'' he explained. "I used to have dreams about growing up, getting into trouble and having to ask my father to defend me. The dream turned into a nightmare when Dad refused, saying 'Chad's always been a stinker. I knew he'd be a bum when he grew up,' or 'Put him in the slammer and throw away the key.' Sometimes the dreams would end with me overcoming my problems and becoming a famous lawyer, someone my dad would be proud of.''

Chad paused. He knew this was the appropriate time to tell Kelly that his problems had ended, he had become a lawyer, and ultimately had changed professions. But by doing so he'd break the personal vow he'd made, and Kelly would realize he had a good deal of money. He mentally weighed the pros and cons of the situation and decided not to say anything.

He felt confident Kelly's estimation of him would rise if she knew he was a success, but he didn't want his personal worth determined by his status in the business world or the size of his bank account.

Skipping over important details, he concluded, "I disappointed both my parents by diligently trying to please them. When Dad died, Mother told me that most of all he wanted me to be my own person—to do what pleased me—to do what made me feel good about myself. Quite simply, I learned how to be happy with who and what I am. What others think doesn't matter." Chad crooked his forefinger under Kelly's chin and turned her to face him. "Good advice?"

"Maybe," Kelly responded thoughtfully, sensing he'd skimmed over relevant facts. "You've left out part of the story, haven't you?"

"I wasted precious years of my life proving myself to other kids, to my parents and, on rare occasions, to a few women. Never again, Kelly. No pop quizzes. I want what you freely give to Wiggles—unconditional love, the kind that allows for shredded nylons."

Upon hearing his name, Wiggles sat up, cocked his head and whined. Intensely involved in each other, neither Kelly nor Chad saw or heard him. As Chad's lips lowered to Kelly's, Wiggles yawned and stretched, then trotted off to find a place to take a nap.

Kelly yielded to the pleasant sensation of Chad's kiss. Her arms went around his neck; her body expressed the vast yearning within her. In one smooth motion, he lifted her across his lap. He kissed her gently and then with growing ardor until she could hardly breathe.

When he finally lifted his head, she read the desire and frustration in his eyes. Mere kisses weren't enough for either of them.

He cupped her face, and he whispered, "I didn't want to fall in love with you. I thought devoting three or four nights to fun and games with you would be enough, but I was wrong." He felt her pulse beating hard and fast beneath his fingers. "In my arrogance,

I thought it would be fun for the teacher to fall for the class clown instead of the other way around." His sigh sent shivers of awareness through her body. "That's not something I'm proud to admit."

"I've known from the day you walked into my classroom and Christy introduced you as Uncle Charming that you could break my heart if I'd let you," Kelly confessed. "At first sight I decided you were a handsome, conceited philanderer. I tried to keep away from you."

Nonplussed by her admission, Chad grinned. "I'm persistent. If Shannon hadn't been in the hospital I'd have built an igloo in your front yard and moved in. I know a good thing when I see it."

"I've always had a weak spot for men who have to be restrained for burning kissability," Kelly teased, nuzzling her lips against his neck. Her hand centered on his chest; his heartbeat steady and strong. "You intrigue me."

"How?"

"You act the clown, but underneath you're extremely sensitive."

"Aside from my sister, you're the only woman who's seen that side of me. I'm usually considered a good-time Charlie."

"Wanna trade reputations? Everyone—my family, Trudy, Tom—they all think I'm one step away from becoming an old-maid schoolteacher."

"That's easily explained. They've never kissed you." He clamped his lips closed and dropped a stingy peck on her cheek. "That's how schoolmarms are supposed to kiss."

"Apple-polisher," Kelly said, please by his compliment.

His lips touched the hollow of her throat. "I love how you kiss. Sweet shyness mixed with fire and passion. A heady combination. One that leaves a man craving more."

Kelly didn't know what to say. She could have told him that he had awakened that fire and passion the first time he'd kissed her. She could have told him that kissing him made her warm and achy. She could have told him dreams of him kept her awake long into the night.

She was unaware that her fingers were fidgeting with the top button of his shirt until it was unbuttoned. The feel of his chest hair came as a mild, pleasurable shock. His fingers closed over hers when she started to put her hand in her lap.

"Touch me, Kelly." With his free hand he unbuttoned his shirt to the waist. "Please."

She barely hesitated before once again raising her hand to that sun-kissed blond hair. His skin was tanned and sleek. His nipples were dark in the shadow of his shirt. Her inquisitive fingers delicately followed the path of springy hair across the muscular swell of his chest, then moved over his shoulders, peeling Chad's shirt down his back.

He was as beautiful as she knew he'd be.

"Kelly, sweet Kelly. Kiss me."

Their mouths met, tongues thrusting, tasting. His hand stole under the ribbing of her angora sweater, moving from her rib cage to the hollows under her arms, then back again and again. Only when he heard a low sound from the back of her throat did he let the heel of his hand caress the underside of her breast.

Kelly didn't hesitate when she felt the front clasp of her bra part. Without giving her actions a second thought, she pulled the sweater over her head and tossed it aside. One shrug of her shoulders and the barrier of cloth from the waist up was gone.

Ever so slowly, Chad pulled her against his chest. Good Lord in heaven, he thought the instant her rosy nipples touched him. He squeezed his eyes shut at the exquisite torment of continuing slowly until she was flattened against him. To prolong the sweet agony, he moved her from side to side.

A flood of passion washed through him. With her on his lap, there was no hiding his masculine reaction.

"Kelly, we'd better stop," he said, his voice almost a groan.

Unsure of herself, she asked, "Am I doing something wrong?"

"Wrong? Woman, you're perfect. Too perfect."

She bit her lip in confusion as he pulled away from her. Trudy's accusation rang in her mind: *You're too perfect for mere mortals.* Was Chad rejecting her for the same reason? She wanted to scream a denial.

His eyes opened until he could see the look of dismay on her face. "Sweetheart, I want you," he told her. "Here. Now. On the sofa. On the floor. A dozen times." He cupped her hip and pulled her against his hardness. "This is no laughing matter, even for the class clown."

She had to let him know she was far from perfect. "Then you'll have to teach me what pleases you," she whispered. "We'll have to practice over and over until I get it right."

Her arms slipped around his neck. One arm around her waist, the other at the bend of her legs, he moved to the edge of the cushion. "Lesson one: What pleases you pleases me."

Balancing her in his arms, he rose to his feet. With unhurried steps, he carried her toward her bedroom. He needed time to cool down.

Dutifully she quoted him, "What pleases you pleases me."

"That isn't quite what I meant. Let's drop the pronouns. What pleases Kelly pleases Chad."

"I like that lesson. Any more?"

"Yeah. Lesson two: Do what comes naturally."

She nibbled a love bite on his neck. "Does that mean I can do anything?"

"That's Lesson three: Forget the rules. Nothing you do will be wrong." He pushed the bedroom door open wide and crossed to the bed. "And the last lesson is the most important. Lesson four." He lowered her to the flowered coverlet and eased down beside her. "Making love with someone dear to you is fun. It makes your soul happy."

He smiled and then kissed her. Somehow she knew she'd never forget that kiss. It was tender, poignant, reverent and altogether wonderful.

He hadn't said he'd loved her; he'd showed her. Each caress, each touch, told her far more than words. Intuitively he knew she was modest. Although he wanted to turn on the bedside lamp, he didn't. Although the pounding need he felt demanded instant gratification, he moved slowly, carefully, cherishing her.

He wanted to shout that he loved her, wanted to scream it, sing it, but his fear of wanting too much, too soon kept him from uttering a sound. He didn't want to overwhelm her.

She loved him so much Kelly felt as if she'd burst, but her fear of not pleasing him kept her silent. She was sure he thought she was a slow learner, a timid lover.

Their remaining clothes seemed to magically disappear. There was no bumping of elbows, noses or knees, no struggling with buttons, zippers and snaps. Only soft whispers of encouragement from Chad and the feel of his hands stroking her, making her passion build to a feverish pitch.

Kelly followed his example.

His kisses ranged from playful to passionate, as did hers. His hands explored the planes and hollows of her body seeking hidden areas of pleasure. Circling his nipple with the tip of her tongue, she thrilled to feel it harden. She delighted in the strong, velvety feel of his skin, the strength of his body against the softness of hers. They had been created for each other, she was sure. And they'd been made for this moment.

She learned her lessons well. Her soft moans spurring him on, she clawed at his back, but he didn't notice. When they became one, she screamed with joy and wrapped her legs tightly around him.

Kelly couldn't believe the sensations his passion aroused. Like the moon reflecting the sun's light, she moved with him until time and motion ceased to exist. Then came the explosion. It started as a ripple, an involuntary muscular contraction, and ended with a mind-shattering burst of pleasure.

For long moments, Kelly didn't know what had happened. She smiled, and her eyes stung with tears when she heard Chad say, "I love you, Miz Mallory."

Indeed, her soul was happy.

Ten

The shrill ringing of the telephone pulled Kelly from her pleasant dreams. She raked her hand through her hair as she glanced at the empty pillow next to her. Had she imagined making love with Chad? Could something so wonderful, so real, have been a dream?

As she reached for the phone, a rosy glow swept from her toes to the roots of her mussed hair.

"Mallory residence."

"G'morning, Miz Mallory." Chad's voice was low, intimate, close, as though his head was only inches from her. "Pleasant dreams?"

"Marvelous."

"I didn't want to leave, but I had to be here to help get the kids ready for school." His tone lowered to a whisper. "I didn't want any of the kids running into the spare bedroom and finding it empty. They'd ask too many questions. Also, I dognapped Mr. Wiggles. I figured you'd be rushed this afternoon."

His consideration toward his sister's children, her reputation and her dog charmed her. "Thanks," she murmured softly. "You should have wakened me. I'd have fixed breakfast."

"As Shannon's chief cook and bottle washer, I couldn't see any point in waking you when I knew I'd have to make breakfast for the kids." Chad paused. "After school we leave for Florida?"

"I'm counting the minutes." Glancing at her bed-side clock, Kelly was propelled into action. "Oh, my gosh, I'm gonna be late!" she groaned. "Phillip will kill me!"

"Sorry. I couldn't set your alarm clock without waking you. I'll let you go...for now." Still insecure about how she felt about him, he asked, "I've arranged to fly out of St. Louis at 4:30. Can I pick you up at school?"

"I'm not packed." She jumped from bed and stretched the phone cord as far as it would reach. She was a foot short of her dresser and the closet. "Chad, I've got to go." Calculating the time it would take to pack a suitcase and get to the airport, she said, "I'll meet you at Lambert Field."

"No. I want to—"

"Chad, I don't have time to argue. What gate?"

"That's what I wanted to talk to you about during the drive to the airport." They wouldn't be taking a commercial flight. His private airplane was ready for departure. After last night he'd decided to tell Kelly everything about himself. There was no reason to keep secrets any longer.

She tried to stretch the cord a few inches farther, but couldn't without disconnecting the phone from the wall. "Much as I'd like to listen, I don't have time right now. Please, tell me where to meet you."

"In front of the main entrance."

"I'll see you at 4:30 . . . unless I'm fired. Bye!"

Kelly slammed the phone down and rushed into the bathroom. She didn't have time to think, only act. In ten minutes flat, she'd taken a shower, brushed her teeth and thrown on a sapphire-blue woolen dress.

She fumed at each traffic light as she combed her hair and put on her lipstick. Don't let this be another Monday, she silently prayed, knowing the day the children were dismissed for a holiday was bound to be hectic enough without her being a nervous wreck.

Once she'd parked her car she did the hundred-yard dash to the front door. She didn't have time to punch in at the time clock and get to her door to stand duty. Deciding hall duty was more important, she hurried to her room.

Phillip was outside her room, eyes glued to his wristwatch, waiting.

"Good morning, Phillip," she said, panting as she unlocked her door. "I made it!" she exclaimed as the first bell rang.

"I stopped by to tell you that if you have any troublemakers, send them to the office immediately.

No monkey business. Today's first priority is to keep the roof on the building. You know how wild these youngsters can get right before a holiday."

She nodded. A passel of first-graders rounded the corner at a dead run, saw the headmaster and slowed to a sedate walk. They didn't want trouble with Phillip, either, Kelly thought smiling to herself.

"Have a pleasant vacation, Miss Mallory."

"You, too."

She breathed a sigh of relief when he strode toward Trudy's room. As usual, Trudy wasn't standing in the hall. Kelly knew she'd be in her room putting the final touches on her lesson. Often Kelly had heard Trudy's views on hall duty: Teachers teach. Energy expended in the hallway was wasted energy.

A six-year-old could have knocked her down with a feather when she saw Phillip leave Trudy's room without a scowl on his face. He wasn't smiling, but he hadn't marched Trudy to her assigned post, either.

After six hours in the classroom, Kelly felt as though she'd been pulled through a knothole backward. The children were antsy; she was antsy. She'd flicked the light switch regularly. One more "gobble-gobble-gobble" while her back was turned and she'd have sent the entire class down to visit the headmaster. They hadn't even been able to begin the name-the-puppy contest.

The only thing that kept her going was the prospect of Chad, long stretches of sun-drenched beach, Chad, balmy breezes, Chad, moonlight swims and Chad.

When her mind wasn't spinning from the frantic demands of the children, she thought of him.

During her free period, she avoided Trudy by staying out of the teacher's work station. She graded papers at the back of the classroom while the children had music class. She didn't want to see Trudy so soon after their argument at the mall. Kelly decided they both needed a cooling-off period.

The final bell caused instant chaos. Even well-mannered children pushed and shoved to be first in line. By no stretch of the imagination could the herd of small bodies moving aggressively toward the door be called a line, she thought. God help anyone who stood in their way.

Kelly noticed that Phillip wasn't anywhere to be found.

Raw nerves provided her with an extra ounce of vitality. Soon she'd be with Chad, winging her way to Florida. Kelly stashed a small stack of ungraded papers in her desk. She wasn't going to spend this vacation working. She'd do it the day she came back. She grabbed her coat, locked her door and headed toward the time clock.

She penciled in her arrival time just as the school secretary, Lydia Sestric, handed her a pink note.

"I'm sorry the message is garbled, but your sister Kathy was near hysteria when she called," Lydia apologized. "And I was trying to act as though she was a parent calling so you wouldn't get another number put in the right-hand corner."

"Thanks, Lydia."

She read the note once, then reread it.

Come quickly. Doctor prescribed immediate vacation for Chuck and me to end postdelivery blues. Teenager from next door taking care of baby for only half an hour after your school dismissal. Sorry such short notice. I know I can count on you. Kathy.

No! Kelly silently screamed. *Why couldn't Kathy call someone else? How could she and Chuck possibly just leave their child without making any definite plans for his care? Why me? Because you always rescue family members, chump.*

No! No! No!

Kelly felt her composure slipping. She couldn't scream and she wouldn't cry. Not here. The room next to Phillip's office wasn't the place for an emotional outburst.

She glanced at the phone. The lines were all lit. Since her sister's house was in Chesterfield, she barely had time to call Chad and tell him she wouldn't be able to go after all. She certainly couldn't be as irresponsible as Kathy and Chuck and shirk her duty to a newborn. She'd have to leave within the next five minutes and drive like a speed demon to get to Kathy's house before the sitter left.

Kelly paced between the desk and the time clock. *Somebody hang up, please!*

The lines remained lit. This is a hell of a time for long-winded conversations. Dammit, somebody hang up!

No such luck.

After waiting until the last possible fraction of a second, she ran from the office, through the front door, to her car.

As she drove, she silently rehearsed what she'd tell Chad. First she'd tell him how disappointed she was to have their plans changed. He wouldn't be happy; she wasn't happy, either. Perhaps she'd be able to make other baby-sitting arrangements for Kathy's newborn. Pauline, her other sister, might be coerced into taking responsibility—for a change, Kelly mentally added. If—and it was a big if—Pauline agreed, she and Chad could catch a later flight. If not, which was more likely, she'd have to make other arrangements. Come hell or high water, she was going to do everything possible to go with him short of leaving the baby with a complete stranger.

"If worse comes to worst, I'll call him, explain and ask him to meet me at my house. Between the two of us, we'll think of something."

Spotting a telephone booth at a gas station, Kelly swerved off the road. It was imperative that she catch Chad at his sister's house before he left for the airport.

"Hello," a child's voice answered.

"Christy?"

"Just a minute..."

"No! Let me talk to your mother!" Too late. She heard the phone fall onto a solid surface. Kelly glanced nervously at her watch. The second hand swept around the face with total disregard for her need for slow motion.

Shifting her weight from one foot to the other, she noticed that the traffic was becoming heavier as downtown workers sped home to begin celebrating Thanksgiving. She couldn't wait much longer. "Christy! Shannon!" she shouted. "Somebody... anybody! Pick up the phone!"

She covered her ear to block the traffic noise and pressed her other hand over the mouthpiece to intensify the background noise at Chad's sister's house. Cartoon music. No one calling for Christy to answer the phone. No footsteps. Kelly knew without a doubt what had happened. Christy's younger sister had answered the phone, then gone back to watch cartoons.

Kelly hung up the phone and jumped back into her car. She hoped and prayed someone would notice the phone was off the hook before she reached her sister's house; otherwise, she wouldn't be able to reach Chad. She could call the airport, but the loudspeaker system couldn't be heard outside where she was supposed to meet him. There wasn't time enough to pick up the baby and make it to the airport before the plane departed.

Grimacing, Kelly realized Chad would think she'd changed her mind at the last minute. He'd probably believe she didn't want to argue about going with him so she'd simply not called and not appeared. He'd be gone; she wouldn't have a chance to explain face-to-face. He'd think she was a liar and a coward.

Kelly racked her brain for another means to contact Chad.

"Trudy! I'll call Trudy when I get to Kathy's house." In spite of their tiff, Trudy was her friend. Kelly could count on her.

She'd grown beyond dreading to ask a favor. Purposely distracting her mind from her immediate unsolved problem, she considered the startling changes she'd made since she'd met Uncle Charming.

Her concept of friendship had changed dramatically.

Comparing friendship to teaching, she realized that they had quite a few common elements. Teachers and students had to interact, activities had to have variety, spontaneity was essential, and the individual personalities had to be taken into account.

She'd squelched interaction with her family and friends by volunteering information before they had a chance to ask a question. Oh, yes, that made her feel needed, safe and secure, but that wasn't enough.

Variety had been eliminated by her good intentions. Her friends knew what she'd say before she opened her mouth. Come to my house for dinner. Let me do the work for you. I don't mind, really I don't. Her litany droned on and on, nonstop. Monotonous, boring, unexciting, she thought, turning onto a side street.

Neither had there been any real spontaneity in her relationship. She'd been as predictable as a one-way road through the Sahara Desert. "Time to add some new signs," she muttered derisively. "Dangerous Curves? Beware Shifting Sands? Billboards? Anything to attract attention rather than be driven over without being noticed."

She'd lost her individuality, too. Everyone simply classified her as Old Reliable.

No more, she promised. She wouldn't kid herself into believing she could change from Old Reliable to Blithe Spirit in one easy lesson. Deep inside, she knew she'd always be there in case of an emergency.

But she had made some small changes already.

She had said no on several occasions. The most amazing thing was that she hadn't been demolished by guilt feelings. Her friends and family had expressed shock, but they hadn't withheld their love because she'd refused to do what they wanted. In fact, she'd discovered they hadn't really cared one way or another. Asking her to do favors had become a habit.

"Habit."

Kathy, the baby of the family, habitually called at the last moment. Why wouldn't she? From the time she'd been in diapers, Kelly had been there. Kelly wasn't a psychiatrist, but she suspected Kathy's postdelivery depression wasn't due to a hormonal imbalance. The baby had displaced Kathy as the center of attention. No longer was she the cute, pampered darling of the family. Accepting total responsibility for another human being was difficult for Kathy. It wasn't an uncommon problem, and Kelly was sure her sister could handle it; she was a Mallory.

The wheels of her car had barely stopped in Kathy's driveway when Kelly darted from the car to the house. She didn't knock, but charged inside.

"I'm Kathy's sister," she called to the wide-eyed girl she nearly knocked down on her way to the kitchen telephone. "I've got to make an emergency call."

She looked at her watch as she dialed Trudy's number. It would take a miracle for Trudy to get to the airport in time to deliver a message, but Kelly had to try. As the phone buzzed, she asked, "What's your name? Where's the baby?"

"Tina." The girl picked up her jacket and school satchel. "Outside in the backyard."

"Alone!"

"The yard's fenced."

Outraged by the girl's callous indifference to her nephew, she slammed the phone down and rushed toward the back door. "How could you?"

"Kathy told me I could leave him outside until you got here," the girl said defensively.

As she darted outside, Kelly wondered what parenthood was coming to when a mother could trot off on a trip, hire an irresponsible adolescent and leave her newborn in the backyard on a frigid afternoon! She was going to clobber Kathy for this stunt.

Frantic, she scanned the postage-stamp-size yard, then ran down the wooden steps at breakneck speed. The only thing she spied was a Saint Bernard, which would have made ten of Mr. Wiggles, loping toward her, its huge tongue lolling out the side of its mouth.

"Where is he?" Kelly shouted, fear making her heart pound. Her face was as white as the unmelted snow.

"Lady, are you some kind of wacko or something?" Tina pointed toward the dog. "That's Babe."

"I don't mean the dog! Where's Jonathan?"

"Jonathan? They're dropping him off at your sister's. Kathy tried to put Babe in a kennel, but there was no room."

"You mean—?" Her eyes darted from the shaggy dog to the teenager. She started to laugh. This kind of crazy thing only happened in the classroom! Laughter was the safety valve that kept her from crying.

"Did you think I put Jonathan outside?" Tina asked indignantly.

Kelly nodded, laughing harder. No wonder the teenager had looked at her as though she'd come straight from the funny farm. "When did they get the dog?"

"About a month ago. My mom told me that Kathy's husband bought the dog so Jonathan and Babe could grow up together—sort of like brothers. Weird, huh?" Tina tossed her book bag over her shoulder. "Hey, listen, I've been paid. The house key is on the kitchen table. Babe's dog food is in the pantry. I've gotta get goin', okay?"

"Yeah." Kelly laughed again to strangle the sob building in the back of her throat. "I'm sorry about the confusion."

"No sweat."

Alone with Babe, tears of self-pity replaced the laughter. She sat down on the back steps and wrapped her arms around the Saint Bernard's neck. It was too late to get to the airport, too late to get a message to Chad, too late to make other arrangements.

"If I didn't have bad luck, I wouldn't have any luck at all," she mumbled into Babe's thick coat of fur.

He turned his massive head and whined. Then he let out a soulful howl.

"I couldn't have said that better myself."

Kelly didn't know how long she sat there feeling sorry for herself. She wasn't mad at her sister. Kathy didn't know she'd planned on going out of town. Undoubtedly her sister had been excited about her own trip; that was what had caused the garbled message. It was a mix-up, plain and simple. She couldn't blame Kathy for expecting her to be there when needed.

"C'mon, Babe. We might as well go to my house. How do you feel about splitting a can of turkey dog food for Thanksgiving?"

Her tread was heavy as she followed Babe up the steps. She checked the house to make certain everything was unplugged, and locked the doors and windows. Babe trotted along behind her like a dutiful host keeping her company as she made her rounds.

Getting Babe into her two-door compact car proved to be a formidable task. She pushed on his hindquarters until she was blue in the face. "You and Trigger are the same size! All you need is a saddle and you could carry me home instead of vice versa!"

Babe's tongue lolled complacently from one side of his mouth to the other. In the spirit of cooperation he curled his tail under his rump so Kelly could get in and shut the door.

Refusing to give up on being with Chad, she kicked several ideas around as she drove. Maybe she could find someone to take care of the dog. She'd done favors for everyone in the neighborhood. If no neighbor would do it, perhaps she could call on Pauline or Trudy.

Okay, supposing she did take care of that giant-size problem, how was she going to get to Florida? It was a holiday. The airlines would be booked solid.

"Except for one unexpected cancellation," she grumbled aloud.

She considered the alternatives to flying. She could drive. Barring breakdowns and accidents, she'd arrive in time to say hello, turn around and drive back. Bad idea.

Maybe she could get a plane ticket to somewhere in Florida, rent a car and drive to Chad's house. Plausible.

Warming up to the idea, she decided to try the airlines for a standby ticket, then she'd call Shannon to get specific directions to Chad's house. She could surprise him. Bad idea. The way her luck was running, he'd take one look at her and bolt the door.

"I'd better wait and call him first," she decided.

But what if he wouldn't talk to her?

"I'll make him listen," she said firmly.

Brave words spoken several thousand miles away from him, she thought. Peacemakers aren't pushy by nature. She'd changed, but not radically.

"If he won't talk to me, I'll arrive at his doorstep unannounced." Remembering what he'd said about building an igloo in front of her house, she murmured, "He'll have to take me in or I'll build a sand castle in front of his for temporary lodging!"

He'd realize his hurt and anger were unjustifiable once she explained what had happened, she told herself. He'd laugh. His sense of humor was one of the things she loved best about him. She counted on it to get them over this rough spot.

By the time Kelly reached her home, she had several major plans mapped out, plus options and alternatives to the options. She wasn't going to give up. This was the most important lesson plan she'd ever put together...and it promised to be exciting!

Eleven

Chad made three trips back and forth between his car and Kelly's house. He'd made short work of the flimsy back-door lock to gain entrance. Later he'd send someone over to replace it. On each trip he carried a large wooden box filled with financial records he'd stored at Shannon's house.

Madder than a hornet, he'd rashly decided to teach Miz Mallory a general lesson in faith and trust. Then he'd get down to specifics about how a man feels when he's stood up.

Half an hour after their arranged time to meet, he'd known waiting was pointless. He could have chalked her up as just a woman who had let fear get the better of her, but he wasn't the sort of man to give up because the going got rough. From experience he knew the consequences of backing away from failure: future failures.

He'd retrieved boxes of old papers from his sister's basement and driven straight to Kelly's house. Page by page he'd make her read the papers his accountant had prepared. "She wants proof that I'm a productive member of society? By God, she'll be reading for the entire vacation!"

He moved his car to an inconspicuous location, returned to the house and turned out the lights. Eventually she'd return. He'd be waiting, and none too patiently!

"Pull it in, Babe," Kelly ordered the dog wedged between the front and back seats. Babe's back legs bicycled as Kelly grabbed him by the scuff of the neck. His big brown eyes expressed benevolent tolerance. "I'd have rented a horse trailer if I'd had any idea this would have happened."

Chad parted the front drapes. His anger ebbed as he watched Kelly. She was in much the same position she'd been in when he'd first seen her. Her backside was swaying provocatively as she pulled and tugged on something in the back seat of her car. What? he wondered. What ever it was, it must be huge.

Babe finally popped from the car like a cork from a champagne bottle. Kelly landed in a snowdrift with one of his front paws on each of her shoulders.

"Get off me, you big oaf!" she screamed.

Babe gave her a grateful chin-to-eyebrow lick and ambled toward the nearest bush to stake out his new territory.

Rolling to her side, then to her feet, Kelly brushed the wet snow from her coat. She knew she'd better get a hammerlock on Babe. Should he decide to water the entire neighborhood, she wouldn't have a prayer of saving the shrubbery. Even tall trees were at risk.

"Inside," she ordered in her most authoritative voice. She pointed to the front steps as she slammed the car door. "Stop lollygaging around."

Obediently Babe followed her command.

Kelly unlocked the door and shooed Babe inside. "You sniff around and make yourself at home. I've got some phone calls to make."

Intent on making arrangements to join Chad in Florida, she headed straight from the foyer to the kitchen. She decided she'd call Trudy first.

"Hello, Trudy?" she said when the phone was answered on the first ring.

A male voice said, "No. She isn't available at the moment."

"Who is this?" She heard the man on the other end of the line clear his throat—a dead giveaway. Kelly would have recognized that sound anywhere. "Phillip?"

She heard his hand cover the mouthpiece and hushed voices in the background.

"Phillip, I know it's you. Just let me talk to Trudy," she yelled. From the living room she heard a low growl. Terrific, she thought, Babe found the spot Mr.

Wiggles made on the carpet, and he knows another dog lives here. "Hush, Babe. You're a guest—mind your manners."

Chad was treed on his stack of wooden boxes. Had he not been curious as to what Kelly planned to say to her best friend, he would have made his presence known. He eyed the massive jaws of the Saint Bernard and said a silent prayer.

Babe sat down back his haunches when his quarry didn't move a muscle; his growl changed to a whine. His floppy ears pricked up when he heard a whispered, "Nice doggy. Good doggy."

"Trudy!" Kelly screamed into the phone.

"Stop shouting, Kelly. You almost broke my eardrum," her friend said.

"Sorry." Kelly wanted to ask about Phillip being with Trudy, but refrained. She'd changed a few of her ideas about friendship, but she still believed a friend should wait for information to be volunteered. Besides, this was not the time to badger Trudy with questions.

"What are you doing in St. Louis? You're supposed to be winging southward," Trudy demanded.

"I missed my flight because I had to run by my sister's house."

"Chump," Trudy said succinctly.

Kelly didn't refute the accusation or bother to explain. "Listen, Trudy, I need a big favor."

"Oh, yeah? What's happened? Did you hear the rumor that Chicken Little is spreading and believed it?"

"Don't joke. The sky isn't falling just because I'm about to ask a favor."

"Ha! You can't kid me. Something catastrophic must have happened."

The house did sort of shake when Babe galloped through it, Kelly thought, half smiling. "I need a dog-sitter for the weekend."

"I thought Wiggles was at Christy's house."

"Different dog. My sister's. Could you take care of Babe for me?"

"Sure. My poodle will love having company."

"Yeah, well, uh . . ." Kelly couldn't bring herself to be unfair. Trudy might renege on her offer, but Kelly had to warn her of Babe's size. "Babe is a Saint Bernard."

"Oh."

"But he's friendly."

Chad looked at the huge dog disbelievingly. Babe remained sitting, but his front paws were perched on the bottom box as if he was daring Chad to make one false move.

"Wait a minute," Trudy said.

Kelly could hear Trudy whispering to Phillip.

"My friend says he'll take care of Babe. He has a big fenced yard." Trudy giggled; then her voice dropped to a whisper. "Considering my dog already tore a hole in his trousers, I'd say he's being very accommodating."

On the verge of making rash promises about the Christmas program, Kelly bit her lip. She'd done favors for Phillip; she didn't owe him anything.

"Thank your *friend* for me, would you?"

"Will do. By the way, I'm sorry I nosed into your personal affairs."

"I'm sorry I was snippy. Friends?"

"You bet. Drop Babe off at my house before you leave."

"Thanks again. Bye."

Before Kelly could hang up the phone, all hell broke loose in the living room. Kelly thought Babe was chewing up the furniture from the sound of splintering wood.

"Babe! Stop that!"

She ran from the kitchen, through the hallway, into the living room. After flipping on the light, her hand automatically covered her mouth. Papers were flying everywhere. Two mysterious wooden boxes had tipped onto their sides. Chad was sprawled in the middle of the room with Babe's paws smack-dab in the middle of his chest.

"Call off the attack dog," Chad ordered her, trying to remain as calm as possible.

"Here, Babe. Let the nice man up. He won't hurt me." The killing glance Chad shot her made her ask, "You won't hurt me, will you?"

"Well . . ."

Babe bared his teeth.

Chad changed the tone of his voice. "She's safe. I don't believe in corporal punishment."

"C'mere, Babe. I'll get you a dog biscuit," Kelly promised. Babe inched backward. "C'mon."

Slowly sitting up, Chad watched as the shaggy hulk obediently followed Kelly into the kitchen. He heard a box rattle, a grateful woof, then the sound of the laundry room door closing. He grabbed a handful of legal papers off the carpet and jumped to his feet.

Kelly returned to the paper-strewn living room, anxious to make explanations. "Chad, I missed the plane because—"

"I know why you missed the plane." His ego was still suffering from the knowledge that she'd used Babe as an excuse. The real reason, she knew, lay in his hands. She believed he was unemployed and unproductive, a worthless member of society. He shoved the papers toward her. Icily he said, "Read the fine print."

"Chad, you're going to laugh when you—"

"This is no laughing matter. Read."

"But—"

"Start reading, lady." He slapped the papers in her open palm. Several sheets fell to the floor. He folded her fingers over those that remained in her palm. "There are a few things you need to learn about me. Now."

Kelly collapsed on the sofa, shaking her head. "But—"

"Now!"

She hadn't the vaguest idea what was going on, but from the forbidding tone of his command, she realized he wasn't going to allow her to get a word in edgewise until she scanned the papers in her hand.

"Okay, okay!"

Legal documents, she quickly surmised. Silently she read the title, "Transfer of Patent Rights." Raising her eyes, she watched Chad pacing in front of her. His expression was grim. Giving up on making her explanation, she began wading through the legal jargon. Nine-tenths of it she couldn't comprehend. From the smattering she did understand, she learned that Chad had been authorized to produce, package and market a European product called Sunshine.

"What's Sunshine?"

"A cologne I'm marketing."

Kelly grinned. Her nose hadn't been wrong; he did smell of sunshine.

"Next page," he ordered curtly. Her smile threatened to melt his resolve to make her read each and every page. She looked so damned cute sitting on the sofa with her legs curled under her. All that kept him from hauling her into his arms and making passionate love to her was the taste of anger that lingered in his mouth. That and the certainty that Babe would chew his way through the laundry room door in a flash if he heard any strange noises.

Sifting through the pages, Kelly said, "I've seen some of these products in the stores."

"Right."

Suddenly it dawned on Kelly what Chad's percentage of the profit could entail. He was a self-made millionaire. He'd traveled to places she'd only read about in geography books. Realizing Chad had conquered the world of commerce single-handed astounded her.

Chad stopped pacing and stared at Kelly. "Can you possibly conceive how degrading it is for a man to have to prove his worth to the woman he loves?"

Like a child with selective hearing, Kelly only paid attention to the word *loves*. "You love me?"

"Do you think I carted this stuff here for physical exercise? It took two strong men and a boy to get them into my sister's house! Knowing you had to have proof of my worthiness gave me the strength to handle them alone."

He'd said his piece. Stalking to the coat he'd thrown over the back of the chair by the window, he muttered, "My pride is too fragile right now to carry on a rational conversation. You can finish reading, then give me a call at Shannon's house."

Kelly knew she had to stop him. *He loves me!* she thought, her heart soaring to new heights. Tossing the papers aside, she bounded off the sofa. She had to stop him at all costs.

"Don't walk out that door, Chad Turner. Babe will think you're a thief unless I tell him differently."

Disregarding her threat, he shoved his arm into his sleeve.

"I wanted to go to Florida with you." She reached for him, but he shook her hand from his sleeve. "Didn't you hear me making arrangements for Babe?"

"Your locating a temporary home for that monster isn't proof you were following me."

Kelly's temper flared. He wasn't going to let her explain; he was deliberately being obtuse. Not only that, he dared to think she was the kind of woman who needed a financial report before committing herself. She would readily admit to having some personality flaws, but being money-hungry wasn't one of them.

Hurt and angry, she pushed her hand against Chad's shoulder hard enough to knock him off balance. He landed, none too lightly, in the chair where his coat had lain.

"You can't bring yourself to trust me, can you? You have to have it in black and white. Notarized! Sorry, you'll have to read it in pink and blue!"

Before he recovered she'd run into the kitchen and was back with her coat. She rummaged in her pocket until she found what she was looking for: the pink slip of paper with the secretary's handwriting. She thrust it under his nose. "Read it. I'm suddenly short on explanations myself."

She watched his head bend. The urge to push the lock of sun-bleached hair back from his forehead had her crossing her arms over her chest.

Chad read the note and pieced together what had happened. He hadn't been stood up because she'd chosen to dog-sit. From the way the note was worded, she'd obviously believed she was taking care of her sister's baby. He couldn't condemn her for doing exactly what he would have done. But . . .

"You could have called."

"I tried. The phone is probably still off the hook at your sister's house. One of your nieces answered but forgot to tell anyone about it."

His dark eyes shone. A wide smile of comprehension lit his face. "You couldn't reach me at the airport, either."

"Right!" She kicked at the papers littering the carpet. "How could you fall for a woman you thought was...a...gold digger!"

Chad threw his head back as genuine, joy-filled laughter pealed from his throat. She honestly, sincerely didn't care two hoots about his income. His doubts had been unfounded.

"Don't you laugh at me, you...you...class clown!" She spun on her heel and headed toward the kitchen. Tears stung her eyes, blurring her vision. "You can leave now!" she called angrily over her shoulder.

Jumping to his feet, a wicked gleam in his eyes, he tore after her. "You love me, don't you? Otherwise you wouldn't be mad."

"You don't know the meaning of the word!" she yelled, changing direction and heading for the safety of her bedroom. He wanted time to think. She'd give him plenty of time. Days! Months! Let him stew in his own juices for years, she thought.

Chad caught her shoulder and spun her around into his arms. "I'm not going to let you go. I've waited too long to find you."

She wasn't going to give him the satisfaction of overpowering her. She stiffened in his arms. "I told you the night you forced me to accept a ride that I was self-reliant. I don't need or want your money."

"You're avoiding the question. You love me, don't you?"

"No," she muttered. At the moment, she meant it. She hated Chad.

"Look at me. Raise those lovely honest blue eyes of yours and take a good long look at me."

Defiantly Kelly looked up. She gasped in surprise at what she saw. If his eyes had twinkled with laughter, she'd have considered slapping him. Or if they'd glittered with triumph she'd have reacted similarly. They didn't. They shone with an inner sunshine that spoke of love.

"Yes," she whispered. "I . . . I love you."

"Irrevocably?"

"Yes."

His hold loosened, but his eyes held hers. "Unconditionally? I could lose everything I own by making one bad deal."

Kelly smiled. "I wouldn't mind it if you had to rely on me for a while. I don't think I can change my need to be needed. It's how I am."

"Never change because of me," he whispered, then covered her lips with his.

The sweet flavor of love passed between them. For long, long moments they held each other, silently communicating their love with kisses.

"Marry me, Miz Mallory?" he finally whispered huskily.

"When?" she asked, nodding her willing acceptance enthusiastically.

"As soon as the three-day waiting period is over?"

Thoughts of being the oldest daughter in a family of six children filled her mind. After her younger sister

had married, her father had expressed a dreamy desire for a big wedding for his remaining single daughter.

But that was what her father wanted, not Kelly. She
wanted to be Mrs. Chad Turner more than she'd ever
wanted anything. By marrying Chad she'd be starting
a new family—one that would take first priority.

"Elope? Where?"

"Florida."

"But we'll never get airline tickets this late." She
gave him a flirty wink then glanced over her shoulders at her rumpled bed. "My memory is in dire need
of a refresher course."

His gaze followed hers, and he smiled. Airplane
tickets weren't a problem. Later, he thought, later he'd
call the airport and rearrange the flight. He unknotted his tie and began unbuttoning his shirt.

"I'm beginning to wonder if I missed my calling."

"You mean you should have been a teacher?" Kelly
unzipped her dress and let it fall to her feet as she
stepped out of her shoes. "You are, but you're only
going to have one student." She caught her breath
when his hands lowered to her hips and rocked them
back and forth. "Me."

"Private lessons?"

He made short work of his trousers, shoes and
socks.

"Definitely." He narrowed the gap between them.
Unclasping her bra, he said, "I don't want you too
self-reliant, though. Occasionally I might help you

with your boots or your clothing. I like undressing you.''

Pleasure sizzled through her as he discarded her filmy underwear and molded her breast in his hand. His thumb caressed the tip, making it turgid. He dropped to one knee, nudging hers apart. As he sucked and nipped her breast, she leaned against him, her head tossed back, her hands tangled in his blond hair.

"Tell me what you want.'' His lips followed the gentle curve of her stomach. ''Tell me.''

''Love me. There.''

Modesty flew out the window as Kelly surrendered to passion.

Her knees melted when she felt his tongue draw a line from her navel downward. He supported her while making passionate forays with his lips and teeth.

Certain the dizzy swimming in her head would cause her to fall, she whispered, ''Hold me.''

In slow motion she slithered down until she knelt in front of him. Her arms cradled his shoulders tightly as her open mouth met his. His tongue thrust boldly inside her. In one swift move, both of them were on the carpet, never having broken the kiss.

Her hands boldly followed the curve of his spine, lower and lower. She heard his groan of approval when she kneaded his taut buttocks. With each thrust, each swirl of his tongue, she could taste his growing ardor.

Chad couldn't wait; Kelly wouldn't let him.

She needed their bodies to be as close as their hearts and souls were. She arched toward him as her hand moved to touch him, guide him inside her. He thrust swiftly, holding her perfectly still while she absorbed the impact. Kelly was filled with an inner peace. Making love with Chad involved far more than seeking a physical release from tormenting desire; it was a perfect bonding between man and woman.

Her eyes wide open in wonder, she saw the look of intense pleasure in his face and the love she knew he felt for her. She arched her hips faster and brought him to ever higher levels of arousal.

Chad felt his control snap. He wanted to last forever, but the movement of her fingers on his hips signaled him not to wait. He thrust harder, deeper, until he felt as though she'd totally absorbed him. They were no longer two people; they were one.

His eyes had been closed; at the last instant he opened them and saw her blue eyes burning with love for him. He heard her moan his name as he climaxed.

Holding her limp body tightly, Chad shifted his weight to her side. In a hushed voice he whispered charming nonsensical phrases that had meaning only for her.

Kelly smiled contentedly, basking in the warmth of his praise. With him close beside her, the peacemaker was finally at peace with herself. Love gave her the courage to do what pleased both of them without fear.

The plush carpet beneath them wasn't the sandy shores he'd promised. There were no swaying palms or tropical drinks. But she couldn't have been happier.

She glanced toward the window as the last rays of twilight changed to darkness. Outside, the temperature was dropping; inside, with Chad holding her, loving her, needing her, she knew she'd always be one lucky lady.

* * * * *

Silhouette Desire

COMING NEXT MONTH

#415 FEVER—Elizabeth Lowell
World traveler Lisa Johansen had never met a man like Ryan McCall before. Their love grew in a sweet summer meadow, but would the bond between them be broken when Rye revealed his true identity?

#416 FOR LOVE ALONE—Lucy Gordon
His new bride woke, remembering nothing, and Corrado Bennoni was glad. Fate had given him a second chance to win Philippa . . . for love alone.

#417 UNDER COVER—Donna Carlisle
Detective Teale Saunders saw an innate honesty beneath con man David Carey's polished facade. When she fell in love with the man she was duty-bound to arrest, she learned that things aren't always black or white.

#418 NO TURNING BACK—Christine Rimmer
Jake Strand had seen her at the worst of times, and Caitlin O'Neill wanted no part of him. But for Jake she had been his turning point, and his hope for the future lay with her.

#419 THE SECOND MR. SULLIVAN—Elaine Camp
Notorious Beau Sullivan wasn't at all like Kelly had expected—and when he started to romance her, she found her ex-brother-in-law hard to resist!

#420 ENAMORED—Diana Palmer
Neither Melissa Sterling nor Diego Laremos was able to resist their passion in the steamy Guatemalan jungle. Torn apart by their families' past, they had to learn trust before they could be reunited.

AVAILABLE NOW:

#409 LUCKY LADY
Jo Ann Algermissen

#410 UNWEDDED BLISS
Katherine Granger

#411 TO LOVE A STRANGER
Beverly Bird

#412 AN IRRESISTIBLE FORCE
Sandra Kleinschmit

#413 BLINDMAN'S BLUFF
Lass Small

#414 MOMENTARY MARRIAGE
Annette Broadrick